Harry Adam Knigh[illegible] and Leroy Kettle.

John Brosnan (1947-2005) was born in Australia but lived most of his life in Britain. He published many books about movies and movie-making (including the particularly well-regarded *Movie Magic*, *Future Tense* and *James Bond in the Cinema*). Three of his horror books (*Carnosaur*, *Slimer* and *Bedlam*—the last two written with Leroy Kettle, all under the pseudonym Harry Adam Knight) were made into movies. Their most successful book was *The Fungus*. Two other horror books were published as by Simon Ian Childer, *Tendrils* (with Leroy) and *Worm*. And they published a collection of humorous pieces—well, they thought they were funny—called *The Dirty Movie Book*.

John also wrote several science fiction novels—the *Skylords* trilogy, *The Opoponax Invasion* and *Mothership*, as well as a range of SF thrillers such as *Torched* (with John Baxter) and *Skyship* and comic fantasy novels *Damned and Fancy* and *Have Demon, Will Travel*.

He wrote a much-liked column for the UK magazine *Starburst* and scripts for the comic *2000 AD*, as well as a range of TV novelisations.

Leroy Kettle (born 1949) also published the science fiction conspiracy thriller *Future Perfect* in 2014 with Chris Evans and, before retirement, worked in the civil service as one of the principal architects of the UK's Disability Discrimination Act.

Both John and Roy first started writing in SF fandom and published humorous fanzines which were enjoyed by the few people who read them.

Harry Adam Knight

THE FUNGUS

With an introduction by
ROY KETTLE

VALANCOURT BOOKS

The Fungus by Harry Adam Knight
Originally published in Great Britain by Star in 1985
First published in the United States by Franklin Watts in 1989
First Valancourt Books edition 2018

Published by Valancourt Books, Richmond, Virginia
http://www.valancourtbooks.com

ISBN 978-1-948405-16-4 (*trade paperback*)

Also available as an electronic book and an audiobook.

All Valancourt Books publications are printed on acid free paper that meets all ANSI standards for archival quality paper.

Cover by M. S. Corley
Set in Dante MT

INTRODUCTION

John Brosnan and I wrote *The Fungus* in 1985, the year that John was best man at Kathleen's and my wedding. (His wedding present of a plaster bust of Prince Charles and Princess Diana marked "Roy and Kathleen" in black felt pen is still in our loft.) *The Fungus* was based on an idea by Kathleen who (thinking there was actually a level to which John and I wouldn't sink) asked if anyone had ever written a novel based on a compost heap. It was, inevitably, about a genetically engineered fungus and things went terribly wrong. As you'll see, my own very limited experiences with athlete's foot form part of the opening sequence—though the other thorough research involved me actually buying a textbook called *Fungus*—and a lot of it is too horrible to summarise. More of *The Fungus* was written by me than some of our other collaborations, though there was a part of the draft I gave to John which he said that even he couldn't pass on to a publisher. Thank God.

The Fungus was our second novel together, after *Slimer* in 1983, though John had used the Harry Adam Knight pseudonym to write *Carnosaur* on his own in 1984. It was our most successful and genuinely well thought of horror novel, despite what seems to be much of the print run of the first British edition (which had a *terrible* cover) still lurking in the loft. Like all our horror books, it was published abroad—France (*L'immonde invasion*), Italy (*Il Fungo*), Poland (*Fungus*—who knew?)—but, most surprisingly, the U.S.A. And in hardback. This was entirely down to Charles Platt, who was working for Franklin Watts, perhaps on a freelance basis, and for some reason thought the book was worth their publishing. It also went on to a U.S. paperback sale (*Death Spore*) and another British edition with Gollancz, but with an even worse cover than the first. At least by then it had had the chance to accumulate through its various editions some cover quotes assiduously collected by the authors from their mates: Clive Barker—"I had a damned good time with this book"; Brian Aldiss—"I loved it and you will find it will grow on you"; every book cover's friend, *Kirkus Reviews*—"Loud, scary sick fun. You will never again go near mushroom soup" and Ramsey Campbell, who actually appears to have read it—"A spectacularly gruesome nasty, written with inventiveness, grisly wit, and considerably more intelligence than almost all its competitors". And, of course, "the new Stephen King" credited to *Starburst Magazine* where John had a column in which he carefully avoided mentioning his own involvement.

On the website Vault of Evil, there is a page (as there is a page devoted to most horror books, I guess) on which a few people write enthusiastically about *The Fungus* in such terms as "*The Fungus* is a great read" and "at times little short of genius". Modesty, on behalf of both John and myself, prevents me from quoting any of this, of course. No, wait.

Both *Slimer* and *Carnosaur* went on to be made into movies—*Proteus* (1995) and *Carnosaur* (1993) (with two sequels). *The Fungus* was never made into a movie, but on a recent trip to Louisville, Kentucky, Kathleen and I were sitting having coffee listening to a street musician near the Seelbach Hotel, which had a ballroom that inspired a young Scott Fitzgerald into setting scenes in a similar hotel in *The Great Gatsby,* when I got an email. From Hollywood. From a producer interested in *The Fungus*. Not a famous or particularly successful Hollywood producer, but then it wasn't a famous or particularly successful book, but, hey, maybe it would pay for our holiday or, at worst, the cup of coffee. And to think that we were sitting only a few yards from where Fitzgerald had got his inspiration. There must be something about great writers and Louisville. However, nothing came of it, but in any event this new edition would still be the best way to experience John's and my work.

John died in 2005. He'd been a close friend for 35 years. We had a lot of fun together, and I hope that you think we put some of it in *The Fungus*.

Roy Kettle
October 2013

Fung'/us (-ngg-), n. (pl. *-i* pr. *-ji*, *-uses*). Mushroom, toadstool, or allied plant including moulds; (Bot.) cryptogamous plant without chlorophyll feeding on organic matter, things of sudden growth; (Path.) spongy morbid growth or excrescence; skin disease of fish.

—from *The Concise Oxford Dictionary*

PART ONE

THE SPREADING

I

London, Tuesday, 6.20 p.m.

By the time Norman Layne arrived home he'd long forgotten the embarrassing collision with the attractive woman in Tottenham Court Road. There were other things preying on his mind now, ranging from the sweaty itch caused by the nylon shirt that Nora insisted was all they could afford, to the lingering fury he still felt towards the black youth who'd played his huge radio as though he owned the train.

And there had been the humiliation of being called back to the ticket collector so that his pass could be checked even though he was always scrupulously honest about paying. But most of all he seethed at having wasted a whole afternoon in that cess-pit of London's West End. He had been specifically told over the phone that Bradford and Simpkins had a forstner-bit brace tang which he urgently needed to continue his carpentry work. But when he got there they then told him they didn't have it. He couldn't understand it. He'd stood there speechless in front of the young and arrogant sales assistant and then realized he was suffering yet another of life's endless, nasty tricks.

Outside he had spat on the pavement in disgust, but then, to his amazement and indignation, he'd got a reprimand from a passing police constable who looked even younger than the sales assistant. Furious, he'd stalked off down Tottenham Court Road, reflecting bitterly that he'd almost been arrested for such a trivial thing while all around him the blacks were fouling up the streets with their noise, their dangerous roller skates, their bikes on the sidewalks and their strutting, swaggering dirty-mouthed ways.

It was then that he'd collided with the tall, blonde woman. It was entirely his fault, he hadn't been looking where he was going. And to add to his humiliation it was he who was knocked off his feet by the impact. He'd fallen hard on his backside and had sat there, the center of attention, for several moments while people had stepped around him with big smirks on their faces. Then the blonde woman had helped him up and apologized but he knew that behind her concerned expression and kind words she was laughing at him too. So he had given her one of his fiercest glares and hurried off down the street without saying anything to her.

And now, finally, he was home. Not that that was much better, but at least it contained a haven where he could escape from all burdens that were his lot. He could even escape from the biggest burden of all—his wife Nora. She had done nothing less than ruin his life. That's all there was to it. He could have been somebody now if she hadn't always been dragging him back.

To avoid her he went round to the rear of the house. At the back door he warily listened for sounds of activity in the kitchen; hearing none he quickly entered and scuttled on through into his workshop. He gave a deep sigh as he switched on the light and closed the door behind him. What meager enjoyment he got out of life was almost all in this room: the cared-for tools, the books of woodwork designs, the finished and half-finished projects, and the lengths of untouched timbers with their distinctive aroma.

He felt a momentary spasm of annoyance that he could not continue with his main job, but there was so much else to do that the room soon exerted its uplifting magic on him and he found an equally satisfying alternate task: the extra-fine sanding of an unfinished cabinet. . . .

He began to caress the already smooth wood with the fine paper. It was a soothing, almost sensual, feeling. He would never have made any sexual association with what he was doing—sex, in fact, had always been low on his list of priorities—but to any objective observer it would have been obvious that he was making love to the wood.

As he rubbed, stroked, and caressed, the tensions of the day began to drain out of him. . . .

Wednesday, 7.07 a.m.

Nora Layne lay in bed wondering what on earth could have happened to her husband. She had dozed off very early the previous night, having treated herself to perhaps one sherry too many that afternoon while the old bastard had been out, and she'd slept right through the night. Yet she was positive Norman hadn't been to bed at all—the covers weren't in their usual tangle caused by his perpetual tossing and turning.

This was odd because even though their relationship was one of mutual detestation, for some reason Norman still insisted on sleeping in the same bed with her. She guessed it was because he wanted to keep up appearances for the sake of the neighbors. Or God. Maybe it was God he was worried about. For years she'd had no idea what was going on in his head except that she played no part in it. Nor did she want to.

So where had he spent the night? On the couch in the living room perhaps? But that was so horribly uncomfortable. He wouldn't have got a wink of sleep.

She smiled to herself at the thought. And now he was probably already up and in his precious workroom waiting for her to get up and make breakfast. Well, she'd be damned if she'd rush to do that today. She was going to make the most of having the bed to herself for a change.

The tension that she usually felt in the mornings was gone, and she was enjoying this momentary rebellion against the dead routine of so many years. A memory seeped into her mind of moments shared with Norman in weekend beds long ago, but it seemed so unlikely and so detached from reality that it soon seeped out again. Small bitter thoughts about her wasted life took its place and she relished the self-pity that accompanied them.

After an hour or so she got up, put on the light-blue, once-fluffy slippers and her faded green dressing gown, and went down to the kitchen. It was empty and there was no sign of the filth that he left on the rare occasions he made his own breakfast. He hadn't even made a cup of coffee.

Puzzled now, she put a glass against the wall and pressed her ear to it. No sound came from the workroom on the other side. Had something happened to him?

The idea didn't alarm her. Life without Norm would be ideal as long as the finances were all right. She wasn't sure about the finances. But if something had happened to him—if he'd had a stroke or a heart attack—she ought to find out as soon as possible. The sooner he was taken away the better. Before he started smelling. She'd heard that the smell of dead bodies was the hardest of all to get rid of in a room, even with the strongest air fresheners.

Tentatively she touched the workroom door with her knuckles, harder when there was no reply. She had to go in then, there was nothing else for it. She hadn't been in there since the time she tidied it and put his tools back in the wrong positions. How long ago had that been? She couldn't remember.

As she opened the door she tensed, ready to retreat at the slightest sound. But she heard nothing. There was, however, a strong musty smell. Emboldened, she stepped inside . . . and almost screamed.

One entire side of the workroom was covered in a thick mold. *Dry rot*, she thought as she stared at it with horror. She loathed the stuff. It had been so expensive to put right in their first home. Norm had shown her the furry yellow and white fungus that had eaten up the floor supports and had then pushed her hand into it as a joke. She shuddered at the memory.

But this growth was much bigger and thicker than the one she remembered. It must have been growing in here for years! The floor, walls and ceiling were coated with the soft, disgusting stuff. It had also grown over what must have been shelves and cupboards but were now shapeless forms under the mold. And the *smell*. It was so bad it almost made her gag.

Why had Norm let it grow? Especially in here, his precious inner sanctum? Then it occurred to her that it might have grown very quickly. In fact it seemed the only likely explanation. Perhaps it had been growing under the floor boards or behind the wall for ages and had just suddenly broken through during the night. Yes, that would explain why Norm wasn't here—he must have gone to get some stuff to deal with it. Some of that fluid that caught in the back of your throat and stank the house out for days.

Well, this was his responsibility, she told herself, and the sooner he got rid of it the better. It was *disgusting*.

She picked up a length of wood and thrust it angrily into one of the bigger mounds of fungus. Unexpectedly, a ripple ran through the growth, then the whole mound moved.

Even worse, it spoke to her.

"Nora," it said in a thick, muffled voice. "Nora . . . It's me!"

And before she could react Norm reached out with two soft, slightly sticky arms and hugged her for the first time in years.

2

Tuesday, 6.15 p.m.

Barbara had thoroughly enjoyed the movie and was sorry it had come to an end. She sat through the credits and was still sitting there when the lights came on, wondering where to go from the theater. She was just about to get up when a tall, attractive blonde woman sat down one seat away from her. Barbara immediately settled back into her own seat.

Very tasty, she thought, *very tasty indeed*. She waited to see if the woman was on her own or if there was a man with her who'd paused to buy popcorn or something. But when the intermission ended she was still on her own, to Barbara's relief.

Throughout the intermission Barbara had kept her under discreet observation. Several times she'd been on the verge of speaking to her, but her usual shackles of anxiety held her back. She never could make the first move in these situations, no matter how much she wanted to. Her fear of rejection was too strong.

So instead she fantasized as to how such a conversation might go, what delights it might lead to—not just for that night but for other nights to come. She desperately needed to get involved with someone else. It would give her the necessary strength to break up with Shirley. Things couldn't go on the way they were for much longer. Yet she couldn't just leave Shirley unless there was someone else to go to. She couldn't stand being alone. Even life with Shirley was better than being alone.

She glanced again at the blonde woman, admiring her fine profile. She looked a proud, strong-willed person. Barbara needed those qualities in a partner. Shirley had them, it was true, but she was also cruel. This woman wouldn't be like that, she was sure.

By the time the lights dimmed, Barbara had decided to sit through the program again. After all, the main feature, a comedy starring Richard Pryor, was very funny and, who knows, something might develop.

During the coming attractions Barbara got up to go to the toilet. As she went past the blonde woman she prolonged the moment of contact with her knees for as long as she could, muttering a soft, "Sorry." In her mind she had inflated that one word into a blatant invitation dripping with tonal suggestiveness, but the other woman said nothing.

On the way back, after some heart-racing moments of anticipation in the toilet, she deliberately stumbled as she passed by. Pretending to lose her balance she tipped towards the woman and for a delicious few seconds found herself embracing her. "I'm *dreadfully* sorry," she said in a loud whisper as the woman took hold of her arm to assist her. "It's quite all right," said the woman in a cool, well-educated voice.

Barbara continued on to her own seat. She'd wanted to sit in one of the empty seats on either side of the woman but that would have been too obvious in such a sparsely populated cinema. So instead, as the film progressed, she kept giving the woman long, lingering glances in the hope that she would catch a reciprocal one. She could still feel the touch of the woman's strong fingers on her upper arm where she'd briefly held her. . . .

But to Barbara's intense disappointment the woman's attention remained fixed firmly on the screen for the whole time. And when the lights came on she was up and gone before Barbara could even think.

Barbara watched her disappear through an exit and sighed. Then, smiling sadly to herself, she got up and slowly left the theater. The evening's fun and fantasies, she realized, were over.

She now faced the prospect of going back to Shirley. Normally that would be bad enough but tonight it would be doubly worse because not only was she late but she was also wearing Shirley's red silk blouse without permission.

Shirley was absolutely impossible when it came to things like that. She was *so* possessive about her clothes and her belongings. And about Barbara, too.

Barbara's steps slowed as she pictured the scene when she got home. *Oh shit*, she thought, *it's almost as bad as living with a man.*

When she tried to open the front door to their Chiswick flat it stopped at the end of the safety chain. *Damn*, she thought, but then shouted as pleasantly as she could, "Shirley, darling! It's me!"

Shirley's voice came out of the hall. "Who's that?"

"*Me*, of course!" answered Barbara, letting just a little irritation creep in.

"Who's me?"

Barbara took a deep breath and forced herself to keep her tone light. "Come on, Shirl, stop playing games and let me in."

Shirley came to the door and peered at her through the gap with an expression of mock surprise. "It *is* you. I could have sworn you were in bed. It's where you *should* be."

"Open the bloody door, Shirley."

"You can't imagine how concerned I was when I got back late and found you weren't here. I almost called the police." She gave a laugh that was brittle around the edges. Then she unchained the door.

"I'm sorry, Shirl," said Barbara as she stepped inside. "I went to the movies . . ."

"When you go to the movies you always go to the late afternoon shows. It's past nine o'clock—so where have you been?"

"It was a good movie so I sat through it again," said Barbara, walking into the living room. She could feel herself blushing as she thought of the blonde woman. She could never hide anything from Shirley.

"That's *very* unlike you, darling," said Shirley sweetly. "And why are you blushing all of a sudden? I can't see where *my* blouse ends and your neck begins."

Barbara's hand flew to her mouth as she remembered the blouse. "Oh, Shirl, I borrowed your . . ."

"Yes, I can *see* that, darling." Shirley gave a light laugh. "Now are you going to tell me where you've been all this time? And who with? Before I get very angry with you, Barbara darling."

"I wasn't *with* anyone, I swear it!" protested Barbara anxiously. "I *did* sit through the movie again. It's the new one with Richard Pryor and you know what a big fan I am of his. It's the truth—you've got to believe me!"

Shirley regarded her thoughtfully for a while, then seemed to accept her story because she smiled and said, "Oh let's just forget all about it. Give us a kiss."

Their lips touched, Barbara's hesitantly but Shirley pressed hard with hers and then thrust her tongue fiercely into Barbara's mouth. Barbara relaxed into the strength of Shirley's passion, and thought that maybe she wasn't so angry after all.

They parted. Barbara grinned, feeling a little foolish. "How was your day then?"

"So-so. I went to the doctors. Some good news, some bad."

"Oh." Barbara paused. She never knew how to handle bad news from doctors. "The good news?"

"I'm not pregnant."

Barbara laughed. Whatever the bad news was it couldn't be serious. "And the bad?"

"I've got an oral fungus infection."

"Oh, you poor . . ." began Barbara and then her face curled up with disgust. She spat on the floor, wiping her mouth on the sleeve of Barbara's blouse. "You bitch! What a dirty trick to play on me!"

Shirley grinned maliciously. "Serves you right. Teach you not to play around behind my back, *and* take my clothes without asking."

Furious, Barbara cried, "Here's what I think of your goddamn precious blouse . . . !" She grabbed the front of it with both hands and yanked hard. There was a ripping sound.

Barbara regretted the action as soon as she'd done it. "Oh, Shirl, I'm sorry . . ."

"You little bitch," breathed Shirley hoarsely, her eyes bright with anger. Then suddenly she lunged at Barbara.

Barbara shrieked and tried to dodge out of her way but Shirley was too fast for her. The impact of their bodies knocked Barbara off-balance and she fell backward onto the floor. Shirley landed on top of her, forcing the air out of her lungs. Barbara struggled hard but Shirley had at least 15 pounds advantage over her and as usual Barbara was quickly reduced to complete helplessness.

Shirley sat straddling Barbara's hips and succeeded in pinning both her arms to the floor, then she reached down and ripped open the red blouse the rest of the way. Barbara struggled even harder, bucking and twisting in a vain attempt to dislodge Shirley. She saw Shirley bend her head down towards her exposed breasts then screamed shrilly as she felt Shirley's teeth bite into her left nipple.

"Oh, you bitch!" she yelled, drumming her heels on the floor as Shirley continued to bite hard into her nipple. "Stop it! Stop it!"

There came a loud thumping from the ceiling above them. It was so violent it made the lamp shade jiggle. Shirley immediately stopped biting her and sat up. In unison they shouted: "Go fuck yourself, you sexist scumbag!"

The thumping increased in volume then abruptly ceased. Their upstairs neighbor, a retired civil servant called Mr. Pickersgill, had made his point for the evening, as usual.

Barbara looked up into Shirley's face which was flushed and damp with sweat. She was breathing hard and her eyes glittered with both excitement and the familiar look of desire. Barbara was feeling very aroused herself and once again she realized why she would find it hard ever to leave Shirley no matter what the provocation. The simple truth was that Shirley was one hell of a lover. No one could ever excite her as much as Shirley did. Certainly no one ever had in the past.

Shirley stood up and then pulled Barbara to her feet. Docilely, Barbara allowed herself to be led into the bedroom. She fell limply onto the bed, rolled onto her back and let Shirley finish undressing her. She enjoyed the roughness of her lover's actions as first her jeans were yanked off and then the rest of her clothes. There was the sound of another rip while the red blouse was coming off but neither of them could have cared less.

When she was finally naked she spread her legs wide in eager anticipation. Shirley stood there for a time looking down at her and Barbara savored the thrill of being so completely exposed to Shirley's hungry, cruel gaze.

Then Shirley was quickly getting out of her own clothes, revealing the long, white, muscular body that Barbara knew almost as well as her own. Of course, in some ways she knew it *better* than her own. . . .

Barbara closed her eyes as Shirley knelt on the bed between her splayed legs. Then she gasped with pleasure as she felt the warm wetness of Shirley's tongue probing the lips of her vagina. The tip of the tongue then moved up to her clitoris and she gave a low, shuddering moan, arching her back as the first pulse of pure ecstasy throbbed through her body.

All thought of the attractive blonde woman in the movie theater had fled from her mind.

Much later, sated and exhausted, they fell asleep in each other's arms. But during the night Barbara had a horrible dream that she was choking. She struggled into semiconsciousness but the choking sensation was still there. Her mouth and throat seemed to be filled with a soft, furry substance. She tried to come fully awake, to cry out, but found herself falling back into unconscious again—an unconsciousness that led to a much deeper oblivion than mere sleep.

When dawn arrived she was still lying there in Shirley's arms. They were joined at their mouths by a pale yellow pulpy mass.

Neither of them was breathing. The venereal fungus which had grown at an accelerated rate throughout both their bodies during the night, and killing them in the process, was visible at their other orifices too. It grew between their legs to form furry yellow diapers and covered their ears like huge, fluffy ear muffs. And though they were both dead, the fungus grew on.

3

Tuesday, 9.45 p.m.

The tall attractive woman with the long blonde hair paid her bill and left the small Indian restaurant in Goodge Street. Naseem the waiter had taken the dishes out into the kitchen and scraped the remains of her meal into a small bin which would later be emptied into the large, round container that sat out in the alley behind the restaurant. The big container would be collected by the pig feed company that had the edible waste franchise for the Goodge Street area.

Naseem was just re-covering the table with another paper table cloth when Derrick Lang and Philip Bell entered. They were laughing loudly and Naseem flinched inwardly. He knew this type of customer only too well.

"Hi, Panjit, old pal," said Derrick Lang, a grossly overweight man of about 30, as he sat down at the table. Lang always called waiters in Indian restaurants Panjit. It was one of his favorite jokes.

"I don't know how you get away with it," said Philip Bell, after Naseem had handed them each a menu and retreated to the small bar at the end of the restaurant.

"They don't mind. Shows them you're not racially prejudiced."

Bell nodded in agreement though he hadn't quite grasped the logic of Lang's theory.

"Watcha'avin?" asked Lang, frowning over the menu.

"Lager, to start with," said Bell, "then I might have a lager and maybe after that a lager."

Lang shook with laughter. Then he called out to Naseem, "Two lagers pronto, Panjit!" He paused for effect then said, "And my friend here'll have two as well!"

They both laughed some more.

"Only kiddin' Panjie boy. A pint each."

Naseem, who was already on his way to their table with two pints, deposited the glasses in front of them and left without a word.

Lang said, "I'm having a vegetable biriani."

"Vegetable!" Bell made it sound as if Lang had made a homosexual pass at him. "You'll be telling me you eat nut cutlets next."

"I read where vegetables help you lose weight," said Lang, a shade defensively. "And because I'm large-boned, meat makes me put on weight quicker than most people."

Bell looked at him. Rolls of fat creased his shirt as if he had a dozen salamis strapped around his body. His buttons were straining to keep the fabric together and several chins sat on top of his neck like a series of miniature stomachs. "Well, yeah, you *do* have large bones, Dekker," he said tactfully.

"Yeah, and the fact is if you eat a lot of vegetables you can also eat as much meat as you like and still lose weight."

"Gerroff."

"No, straight up. I read it in *The Sun*, I think. Or maybe *The Daily Mail*. It's something to do with the vitamins in the vegetables. They make the meat fat burn up without you having to do any exercise."

"How about that."

"You should try it yourself, Phil. You could do with losing a few pounds too."

"Well, maybe," said Bell, even though he knew he wasn't overweight in the slightest.

"You don't have to go all the way at once. You can have, say, a meat madras with a cauliflower bhajee. Cauliflower must have lots of those vitamins."

Bell nodded thoughtfully. Lang took it for agreement and called Naseem over. He ordered food for both of them and another pint of lager each. "You'll thank me for this," he said.

"I will if you pay," said Bell and laughed uproariously.

The evening went quickly as they swapped jokes and solved the various social and political issues of the day. Bell even enjoyed his cauliflower bhajee, but Lang hadn't been so keen on his vegetable biriani this time and consoled himself with the thought of having a doner kebab on the way home.

When they finally lurched, belching and laughing, out of the restaurant it was after 11 p.m. They had each consumed seven pints of lager by then and had reached the stage when everything they said was even more devastatingly funny than usual.

Naseem bore their lengthy farewell routine with the stoicism that any Indian waiter working in Britain must quickly acquire and breathed a silent prayer of thanks when, after a final volley of "Panjits," the two men staggered away.

They walked up to Warren Street station where they went their separate ways, Lang catching the Victoria Line and Bell the Northern.

Lang changed onto the Piccadilly Line at Kings Cross. He got out at Bounds Green and went straight to his studio flat, having decided he was too full of lager for a kebab after all. And anyway there was something he had to take care of rather urgently. All the walking had made his feet noticeably sweaty, and he was worried about his athlete's foot.

He'd suffered from it badly on a few occasions—toes cracking apart, pain like his flesh was being split with a knife—so now he always kept his socks filled with Preparation AF and every morning and night carefully smeared the powder and cream between his toes.

It had always been a matter of some pride to him that he suffered from athlete's foot. It confirmed his belief that within his bulky frame a potential athlete was waiting to get out. And when he succeeded in finally getting his weight down he fully intended taking up some athletic activity. Like squash or badminton. Or maybe sky-diving. Sky-diving didn't involve much running about.

After the nightly foot ritual Lang crawled into bed and switched off the lamp. He was too tired to see if there was anything on TV. He fell asleep almost immediately but slept badly. He tossed and turned in the grip of horrific dreams for several hours and then came fully awake to discover he was suffering an appalling attack of indigestion. "*Goddam vegetable biriani!*" he muttered. "*Never again!*"

And on top of that he was itchy all over, his feet especially. Had the Indian food aggravated his athlete's foot? It never had before.

He lay there for a time hoping the itching would fade, but if anything it got worse. He had no choice but to apply more Preparation AF.

With a sigh he sat up and switched on the light. He pushed back the covers and frowned. Then he laughed. No wonder his feet were itching—he was still wearing his socks.

Then he frowned again. He *had* taken them off. He distinctly remembered doing so. In fact he didn't even recognize these socks. He was positive he didn't own a pair this color—gray with a red pattern.

He reached down to take them off and his fingers sank into the fluffy pulp that was now his right foot.

His heart gave a massive thump, paused and carried on. His flesh crawled with revulsion and his insides seemed to shrink. His fingers, shaking now, fumbled at the other foot. It felt the same—soft and yielding as if it was boneless.

His scream came out as a croak. Then, as he became more aware of the general itchiness all over his body, he tore furiously at his pajama jacket.

"Oh God," he whimpered.

His lower belly was covered in the same gray, red-streaked substance. He managed to undo his pajama pants and, terrified at what he expected to see, looked at his groin and thighs. It was as he feared—from his waist down it was as if he'd been coated in some kind of furry paint that had started to crack. He reached tentatively to touch the mound that now concealed his genitals. It felt like velvet-pattern wallpaper.

"Christ," he moaned, "I've been poisoned . . . that bloody Indian restaurant . . ."

He had to get help, he decided. He got quickly out of bed and took two steps towards the phone before his left leg, riddled with the athlete's foot fungus, snapped at the shin with a sound like a piece of celery being broken.

He fell on his face with a crash that shook the floor and lay there in a state of shock for over a minute. Then, with painful slowness, he started to drag himself toward the phone. His lower left leg remained on the floor beside the bed. And as he crawled he left a trail of crumbling gray powder behind him on the carpet.

4

Tuesday, 10.55 p.m.

The landlord of the One Tun, Eric Gifford, decided to check the Lounge Bar on his way back up from the men's room in the basement. It was, he saw, almost empty except for a few of the regulars. No matter, he'd had a good night's take in the Public Bar, he told himself.

It was then he noticed the tall, blonde woman drinking a red wine by herself at a table near the door. Odd to see a woman drinking alone in this pub, but she looked too well bred to be a whore. Then again, he reflected, you got some unusual types of women on the game these days. He blamed the recession. . . .

He looked at her more closely and then decided he'd seen her before. She wasn't a regular but she was definitely familiar. Maybe she'd only been in the pub once before, but he remembered her face. It wasn't the sort of face a man was likely to forget. She was a looker, all right, and from what he could see of her body it made a good match with her face.

He whistled as he headed back to the Public Bar. Looking at beautiful women always cheered him up. Even at times like this when his bowels were playing up.

It was all the fault of the Yard of Ale competition he'd organized earlier in the evening. He hadn't actually taken part in it, because he was too good, but as usual he'd given a demonstration of how it should be done just to impress the young'uns. Oh, he knew they wouldn't be impressed to begin with but later when they were pouring beer all over themselves or choking or giving up halfway it would dawn on them they'd seen a master of the art in action. And then he'd really rub it in when it was all over by casually downing a *second* yard of ale, which is what he'd done tonight as usual. He'd managed it okay but it had been a struggle at the end, he had to admit. His guts had been giving him hell all day and this had been his fifth trip to the toilet, without success.

He was so constipated he felt like a pregnant elephant. Perhaps he'd better do what his damned doctor kept advising and cut down on the drink. One of these days. . . .

Despite his acute discomfort he pulled himself together as he entered the public bar and began the task of getting people to drink up with his customary diplomacy:

"Come on, you drunken buggers! Haven't you got homes to go to?" he bellowed.

He loved to play the tough landlord and, although the regulars knew it was all a game, the tourists and other drop-ins always looked satisfyingly alarmed when his red-faced, pot-bellied form appeared suddenly in their midst breathing fumes and yelling insults at them. It was always a great way to end the day.

And as a point of principle, when everyone was gone he always helped to clean up. He knew he was often more of a hindrance than a help by that stage of the night but the staff didn't mind. He was quite a good employer as landlords go. Even the girls didn't get too upset when he rubbed his belly against them "accidentally on purpose-like," as he told his friends. They knew he was just having some harmless fun, that there was nothing more to it.

Tonight, however, he didn't feel like rubbing his painfully distended belly against anyone, no matter how young, soft and female they might be. In fact he didn't even feel up to helping the staff, he just wanted to collapse. And so, after a brief clear-up in the Lounge, which consisted mainly of wiping the table where the attractive blonde had been sitting and picking up her glass, which still contained several mouthfuls of wine, he said goodnight to his staff and headed upstairs to bed.

As he climbed the stairs his belly rumbled and he let out a tremendous fart. He was already regretting not being able to resist swallowing the remains of the blonde's red wine before washing the glass. On top of the dozen or so pints of Bottom Draught he'd consumed that evening the small amount of wine could turn out to be the alcoholic straw that broke the camel's back.

He sat down heavily on the big, sagging double-bed, tugged off his shoes then collapsed backward, not bothering to undress. As he drifted quickly off to sleep he thought briefly of Marianne, as he always did at this time, even though it had been eight years since his late wife had shared the double-bed with him. There had been no one else since then.

During the night, as he slept, the live yeasts in the beer that filled his stomach and intestine underwent a remarkable molecular change....

Yeast, the only fungus that grows by budding rather than by producing the long tendrils called hyphae, is also the fastest growing fungus with the theoretical ability to increase a thousand fold in 24 hours. The transformed yeasts in Eric's stomach, however, were now capable of growing at a hundred times that rate.

Which is what they were proceeding to do.

Feeding first on the sugar in the contents of Eric's stomach the yeasts budded and grew at a phenomenal speed, producing more alcohol as a waste product as well as a considerable amount of carbon dioxide gas.

Then, when the transformed yeast fungi had exhausted the supply of sugar within his stomach they began to break down the cells of the stomach wall and the intestinal linings. If Eric had been awake it would have felt as if his internal organs were on fire but, mercifully for him, the large amount of extra alcohol created by the yeast had already put him into deep unconsciousness.

Then, slowly at first but then much more quickly, Eric Gifford began to ferment.

And as he fermented his body expanded...

Just after 4 a.m. Eric's staff were woken by a muffled but powerful explosion which seemed to come from their employer's bedroom. All five of them gathered in the passageway outside his room. They banged on the door and called out his name but there was no response. Finally the bravest among them opened the door. Immediately a horrifically strong yeasty stench poured out of the room, making them gag.

Choking, two of them reluctantly entered the room and switched on the light. The others crowded around the doorway.

To begin with none of them could comprehend what they

were looking at. Then one of the girls screamed and ran down the passageway.

Eric Gifford's head, one of his arms, and both of his legs still lay on the bed but the rest of him was spread fairly thickly over the ceiling, walls and floors.

And in the depression in the bed created by his 250-pound bulk over the years lay a bubbling and seething white mass.

Wednesday, 2.15 a.m.

Naseem and his brother Dinesh had managed to clear the last customer out of the restaurant by 2.00 a.m. and were now helping Maheed, their uncle, clean up in the kitchen.

Naseem was exhausted. He disliked working these long hours but it was the only way he'd be able to save enough money to return to Delhi for good. His other uncle, Makund, who owned the restaurant, as well as two others, was not an easy man to work for but he paid well if you worked hard.

His brother Dinesh was humming a new Indian pop song as he finished scouring the stove. Naseem regarded him wearily, envying him his energy and his continual high spirits. Dinesh was a mystery to him in many ways. For one thing he seemed quite content to stay on in England and had hopes of opening up a restaurant of his own. To Naseem the idea of spending the rest of his working life in this depressing, gray country and waiting on its increasingly surly and ill-mannered inhabitants was profoundly depressing.

He remembered the two men he'd served earlier that night, the fat one and the thin one, and scowled. "Pigs," he muttered. "Why do we get so many pigs in this place?"

Dinesh laughed. "Because it is place that makes pig food." He gestured at the food scrap container which was full up again. Naseem sighed and went and picked it up. "The pigs that eat *this* are probably better behaved than the ones who sit in the restaurant."

He carried the bin out the back door and into the alley. He was just about to empty the smaller bin into the bigger one when he paused and blinked several times. But the apparition refused to go away.

The big cylindrical bin was covered with huge growths that looked like giant toadstools. They were about 18 inches high and a foot wide. They were sprouting out of the top of the bin and down its side like frozen beer foam.

Naseem stared at them in amazement. They hadn't been there when he'd last emptied the kitchen scraps . . . when? Less than three hours ago?

He called to the others. The tone of his voice brought them out at a run. They reacted to the sight in the same way he did.

After a long pause Dinesh said, "What *is* that stuff? Where did it all come from?"

Naseem shook his head. "I don't know. It wasn't here before. It's grown very suddenly."

They both looked to the older man for enlightenment, hoping that their uncle had encountered something like this in the past. But he seemed as astonished as they were. "They're like mushrooms. Like giant mushrooms," he said slowly.

"More like toadstools," said Naseem doubtfully. "Toadstools can grow this big, can't they?"

Dinesh disappeared into the kitchen and returned wielding a broom. "We must destroy them."

"No, wait," said Naseem, stepping in front of him. "Perhaps we should call the Health men. Those things are not normal."

"The Health men would close us down," said their uncle. "And my brother would have our skins. We cannot tell anyone about this." He nodded to Dinesh. "Go on, get rid of them."

Dinesh pushed past Naseem and began to energetically attack the growths with the broom. As the broom struck them the larger fungi burst with a dry popping sound, releasing a faintly luminous cloud of green powder. Very soon the whole alley was filled with the dust and all three men were covered with it.

Dinesh continued with his flailing until all the growths were gone and only powder remained. This he swept up and dumped into the big container. By 3.00 a.m. no visible trace of the fungi remained, either on the ground or in the air. A breeze had sprung up and the cloud of tiny fungi fragments had been carried away.

By 3.30 a.m. the billions of particles were spreading over the West End of London . . . and beyond.

5

Tuesday, 5.20 p.m.

How it began . . .

It was the happiest day of Jane Wilson's life. As she stood there in the laboratory cradling the organism in her arms she couldn't remember ever feeling this elated before, even at the birth of her son Simon.

She was holding a specimen of *agaricus bisporus*, a species of fungus more commonly known as a "cultivated" mushroom. But it was no ordinary specimen. For one thing its pileus, or cap—which was resting against her left breast—was over a foot in diameter, and the stipe, or stalk was over two feet long and seven inches thick. Altogether it weighed nearly four pounds.

It differed in another more important way from an ordinary *agaricus bisporus*—this mushroom was protein rich, yielding almost as much usable protein per gram as poultry flesh.

It was the result of seven years hard work and research but at last she'd succeeded. Two hours ago the giant mushroom she was now hugging to her breast had been a tiny spore of almost microscopic size sitting in its tray of nutrient jelly. And now, just a short time later, it was big and protein rich enough to provide one person with enough food for a day.

Jane felt tears rolling down her face. No one had a right to be this happy, she told herself. "Oh baby, *baby*," she whispered to the fungus, hugging it harder, "You are beautiful, and you're *mine . . . all mine*."

Then she caught a glimpse of her reflection in the glass wall that sealed off this section of the laboratory and felt momentarily embarrassed. "Hell, I look like the Madonna with Child," she muttered to herself, ". . . positively downright *beatific*."

It was time to stop acting like an emotional fool, she decided, and start behaving like a scientist again. The self-congratulations could come later. There was still work to do.

She took the mushroom to a nearby table and laid it out,

almost reverently, in a large enamel tray. Then, with a scalpel, she cut a small section out from the edge of the cap. It wasn't an easy thing for her to do—to mutilate her perfect creation in this way—but it had to be done.

She turned the section over in her hands and examined the gills on the underside of the cap. Her heart sank a little. The section was enlarged enough for her to see with the naked eye the hymenium covering the surface of the gills. The hymenium is the substance from which the basidium grow—the basidium being the micro-organisms that form the mushroom spores. An ordinary mushroom can eject spores at the rate of half a million a minute during the two or three days of its active life but Jane could see that the hymenium on this super-sized specimen was under-developed.

Nervously, she sliced a small sliver from the gill section and placed it under a microscope. Her heart sank still further. The microscope confirmed her fear. The hymenium was not forming any spore cells. She sighed and rested her chin on her hands. So her triumph was not yet 100% successful. She, and her small team of assistants, had succeeded in creating a giant, fast-growing, protein rich mushroom but the genetically engineered organism that produced these traits obviously inhibited the mushroom's reproductive cycle.

Originally Jane and her team had attempted to reach their goal by genetically altering the mushroom spore cell itself but nearly four years of effort produced no worthwhile results. Unravelling the genetic code of an organism even as simple as the *agaricus bisporus* fungus was a monumental task that Jane finally realized they lacked the resources to successfully accomplish. Unless she was given an extra 20 people and unlimited funds—both of which she knew were out of the question—they might still be trying to crack the code in 10 years' time.

So Jane had decided to try another approach. Instead of trying to alter the whole organism genetically she instructed her assistants that from then on they would approach the problem from a different angle and concentrate on only *one* aspect of the mushroom's metabolism. They would isolate the enzymes that helped to control the mushroom's size, growth rate, and protein retention level, and then try and modify them accordingly.

Isolating the specific enzymes—and fortunately there were only two—took a further 12 months. Jane and her team then began to try and build an artificial enzyme that would supersede the functions of the two existing ones within the *a. bisporus* cells and accelerate the relevant processes at least a hundred-fold.

It had been a long and painstaking job recombining the DNA strands of the enzymes in an attempt to create the desired chemical structure that would in turn act like a supercatalyst within the mushroom. Enzymes, however, are extremely unstable; their crucial three-dimensional structures often falling apart in only a few hours.

To overcome this problem Jane and her team were obliged to build, finally, a micro-organism that was more like a virus in structure than an ordinary enzyme. But even when they'd succeeded in creating this unusually stable macro-enzyme they had yet to hit upon the precise chemical combination of the four basic chemical sub-units of deoxyribonucleic acid, DNA, that would produce the desired effects in the mushroom.

So the last 18 months had been spent in testing different versions of the enzyme on the *a. bisporus* spore cells. Each manufactured enzyme had differed from the others in only the smallest and subtlest ways in their atomic structure but when introduced to the spores they produced widely differing changes in the mushrooms, many of them drastic but none of them the required ones. Until now.

Now, with Enzyme Batch CT-UTE-8471 they'd hit the jackpot. Or almost. . . .

Jane regarded the giant mushroom thoughtfully. Even though the enlarged specimen's reproduction system had been retarded in some way by the accelerated growth process it was still a considerable and historic achievement. And it was possible that the reproductive system had merely been slowed down by the modified catalyst. Tomorrow she would grow another specimen but leave it attached to the mycelium—the fungoid equivalent of roots—for a longer period.

Even if reproduction had been completely inhibited by the new enzyme it was possible that further modification to the enzyme structure would solve the problem. And even if it didn't it wouldn't seriously affect her achievement in the long term, she now realized. If the enzyme could be manufactured in large quantities cheaply—and she saw no reason why it couldn't be—then it would simply be a case of applying it to the mushroom cultivation trays containing ordinary *a. bisporus* spores, perhaps in the form of a spray, in order to grow any number of the giant variety.

She leaned back on the stool, straightened her back and stretched her arms above her head. She grinned, her feeling of elation returning. Okay, so she hadn't been 100% successful but she was so close it didn't matter. She *had* created a new and plentiful source of cheap protein that would greatly alleviate the world food shortage. And—who knows?—might lead to a Nobel Prize.

Of course she would have to share the award with her three assistants, Rachel, Tod and Hilary . . . what a shame for them they hadn't been in the lab to witness the actual moment of success but she had sent them all home at lunchtime. They had been working around the clock for the previous 24 hours testing a new series of enzyme batches. All had proved negative and it was only on a whim that Jane, by then alone, decided to try just one more variation before going home herself.

She stood up and smiled at the mushroom. She would leave it there on the tray for them to see when they arrived in the morning. The expressions on their faces would be something to remember.

In the meantime she was going to savor her triumph all by herself. It would be exclusively hers for the next 18 hours or so.

She felt a momentary pang that she couldn't share it with Barry but all that was finished now, probably for good. True, it was supposed to be a 'trial' separation but she couldn't see them ever getting back together again. The last year before the break-up had been hell. She knew she was partly to blame—her involvement with her research *had* become obsessive—but Barry could have been more supportive instead of acting like a spoiled brat. He knew how important her work was, not just for her but possibly for the whole of mankind, yet he persisted with his ridiculous behavior.

The real problem, she now realized, was that he deeply resented the success she had made of her career. Mycology, after all, had been his field too but it was she who had attracted all the attention, right from the start, with her Ph.D. paper *The Relationship Between Fungi and Mankind: Areas of Potential Exploitation in Agriculture and Industry*, and subsequently received the research grants and a department of her own while he had just plodded on doing basic research.

Well, perhaps he was happier now writing his childish thrillers over in Ireland. She knew his books were beginning to enjoy a popularity of sorts—but what a waste! Imagine spending your time producing escapist fantasies for emotionally retarded adults when you could be doing something useful with your life.

She gave the mushroom one last lingering look then went to the door. It slid open at the touch of a button. She stepped through into a small room enclosed by frosted glass. As the door slid shut behind her there was a hissing sound from above. A harmless but powerful anti-bacteria gas was being fed into the room. She began to strip off her clothes—the rubber gloves, the plastic cap, the face mask, the long white gown, the paper briefs and then finally the plastic overshoes and slippers. The reusable items went into the sterilizer, the non-reusable into a small electric incinerator.

Then she stepped into a shower cubicle and turned on the water, which also contained anti-bacteria agents.

As she soaped herself thoroughly she gave her body an indifferent inspection. Despite her 31 years and two children it was still a good body with long, well-shaped legs, firm stomach and large but equally firm breasts. Once she had been proud of her body but now her looks, and even her sexuality, rarely impinged on her consciousness.

This had been another point of contention with Barry. "Making love to you is like making love to the mattress," he had accused her. "And you know why? Because you're sublimating your sex drive in your damn work! Your body may leave the lab occasionally but your mind stays in there 24 hours a day. All you're ever really thinking about are your precious fungi. Hell, the only way now I could turn you on would be to dress up as a fucking fungus myself, *phallus impudicus* preferably."

She had told him he was talking nonsense but deep down knew there was some justification in what he'd said. But it couldn't be helped—the work *had* to be continued at that fast pace. She promised herself that once she achieved her goal and the pressure lessened she would try and make it up to Barry. But, of course, the marriage had collapsed well before that had happened.

By the time she'd finished showering her thoughts had left Barry and returned to the fungus lying on the lab table. As she walked naked to a second glass door and then stepped through into a small changing room she was thinking that tomorrow she would try the enzyme on a specimen of *agaricus campestris*, the ordinary field mushroom which was very similar to the cultivated variety but actually a different species. It was possible that the reproduction-inhibiting factor might be only present in *a. bisporus*. . . .

The thought cheered her up still further as she dressed and began to dry her long, blonde hair with a portable drier.

It was then she noticed the cut on her right forefinger. It was a small incision on the very tip of her finger, extending at right angles from the end of her fingernail for just over a quarter of an inch. As she held it up for a closer look a small drop of blood oozed out. Automatically she put the end of her finger in her mouth and sucked. . . .

Frowning, she wondered how she could have cut herself. Then she remembered removing that sliver from the gill segment for the microscope. She must have nicked herself with the scalpel. Oh well, it didn't matter; the cut would have been well and truly cleaned by both the antiseptic gas and water. Not that there was any chance of picking up a dangerous infection from anything in her lab. Despite all the elaborate safety precautions, which were imposed on all the Institute's genetic engineering facilities no matter what the nature of their work, she knew that there was nothing potentially harmful among any of the artificial microorganisms that she and her team had created over the years.

Or so she believed. . . .

Unknown to her, several thousand microscopic mushroom cells still remained in the cut and under her fingernail. They were dead or dying but the virus-like enzyme, which had been designed to survive for as long as possible, was still active within all the cells.

And while the enzyme wasn't directly harmful to human life its indirect effects were to prove, very swiftly, catastrophic.

Humming to herself Dr. Jane Wilson finished dressing and made her plans for the night. Though she hadn't slept for the last 36 hours she was too excited to go home to bed. No, she wanted to celebrate, and she'd celebrate by having her first self-indulgent night out in years. She would go to a movie, perhaps—preferably a comedy—then have an Indian meal and after that go to a pub and get quietly drunk. She would do all the things that she and Barry used to enjoy doing when they first met.

Damn, she was thinking about him again. She wondered if she should give him a call when she got home and break the wonderful news. No, he'd probably be typing away over there in Ireland even at that late hour—wearing his stupid ear-plugs—and would accuse her of interrupting his "flow." That was if he even bothered to answer the phone.

No, she decided, she wouldn't call him. He could read about it in the papers.

She left the Institute of Tropical Biology at 5.18 p.m. and a short time later was walking down Tottenham Court Road. At 5.22 p.m. she bought a newspaper to check the cinema listings. She was looking at the paper when she collided with Norman Layne . . .

6

Wednesday, 5.55 a.m.

Dr. Bruce Carter swore when he saw what time it was. A phone call before 6 a.m. meant two things: trouble, and not enough sleep to cope with it.

He reached out for the phone on the bedside table and picked it up. "Emergency," said the familiar voice of the Duty Officer, confirming his fears. "Get to the Middlesex Hospital as quickly as you can."

Carter didn't bother asking what had come up. Even if the Duty Officer had the details he would be reluctant to give them over the phone. Security in the civil service was continually getting tighter under the Thatcher regime and a whole new set of regulations governing what it was permissible to discuss by telephone had recently been issued. The weather was about the only safe subject left.

He forced himself out of bed and stumbled into the bathroom. The sight of his face in the mirror was enough to jolt him into full wakefulness. He looked like his father. Or rather what his father had looked like at 50. The trouble was that he was only 43.

I'm working too hard, he told himself as he threw cold water on his face and then began to clean his teeth. *At this rate I'll be dead of a heart attack long before I reach retirement age . . . just like Dad.*

And yet he enjoyed his job, in spite of the long, unsocial hours, and the pressures, and certainly didn't want to be transferred into a less strenuous department. He knew he'd be bored doing anything else.

Dr. Bruce Carter was a medical investigator for the Home Office. His duties ranged over a wide area, dealing with everything from rabies control to tracking down the origins of outbreaks of communicable diseases like typhoid, TB and the like. He was also an expert on toxins and was often called in on suspected murder cases. All in all it was a fairly exciting and challenging job that didn't follow any particular routine. He hated routine but he loved challenges.

He parked his car in Goodge Street at 6.25 a.m., pleased with himself at how quickly he'd made it into town. As he got out of the car he was aware of how quiet it was at this time of the morning. If only it was always like this, he thought, as he hurried toward the entrance of the Middlesex Hospital.

On the way he noticed something odd; growing out of a drain next to the footpath was a clump of the biggest toadstools he'd ever seen. They were white, spherical things almost the size of footballs. He was tempted to examine them more closely but there wasn't time. Later perhaps.

Inside the building he gave his name to the receptionist who, predictably, couldn't find it on her list. Carter was patient. "Try looking under 'C'," he suggested politely.

She eventually found a Dr. Bruce "Cowper" on the list and agreed, a shade reluctantly, that it was probably him. "You're to go to the Contagious Diseases Ward, Block C, Level two and ask for a Dr. Mason. Take that lift there and press the button marked two. Then . . ."

But Carter was already running for the lift. "Thanks," he called over his shoulder. "I know the way."

On the second floor he encountered a nurse heading toward him from the direction of the Contagious Diseases Ward. The look on her face disturbed him. Her expression was one of shock. It was rare for a nurse to display her emotions that way, no matter what she might have witnessed. Carter began to get an unpleasant feeling in the pit of his stomach.

He went through the door marked "Contagious Diseases" in big red letters. Beyond, in a short passageway, sat a nurse at a desk. There was another nurse with her, talking in a low voice. They both looked up at him as he entered. Their eyes had the same expression of dull shock as the nurse he'd passed outside. His feeling of foreboding increased.

He gave them his name and one of them took him along into a small room. She handed him a plastic anti-contamination suit and told him to put it on. He stared at the suit with surprise. He'd worn such clothing before, but only rarely, in extreme situations.

The last time had been during the investigation of a suspected escape of smallpox bacillus from a research lab.

He gestured at the suit's self-contained oxygen supply and said to the nurse, "Rather drastic this, isn't it? Isn't your patient in an isolation unit?"

Tersely she said, "There's more than one of them and, yes, they are in isolation units, but Dr. Mason advises the use of the suit just the same."

He said nothing more as he climbed into the suit. When he was ready she checked the seals then indicated another door. "Go through there. You'll find a door at the end of the passageway. Dr. Mason will be waiting to meet you beyond it."

"What's the problem?" he asked her, his voice distorted by the plastic helmet.

"I think you'd better let Dr. Mason explain the situation," she said and then left the room.

Carter paused for a while, then went to the door she'd indicated. He was positive now he was not going to enjoy what lay at the end of the passage.

Dr. Mason, similarly attired like an extra from *Star Wars*, met him as he stepped into a small ward that was all pristine whiteness and glittering medical equipment. Carter had met Dr. Mason once before at an emergency meeting to discuss the AIDS problem about a year and a half ago but knew him mainly by reputation. And that was very impressive indeed.

"Ah, Dr. Carter, I'm glad you made it here so quickly," said Mason. "I'm afraid we have quite a serious problem on our hands . . . *quite* a serious problem."

Behind the plastic of his helmet Mason's round, sweat-covered face was haggard with strain. Carter glanced past him at the six beds the ward contained. Each bed was covered by a plastic tent. In four of the tents he could make out vague shapes.

He peered hard at the nearest bed/tent. The patient within it seemed to be entirely covered in thick bandages. Yellow bandages. He went nearer. Mason followed.

"What happened to him? Or is it a her? Those bandages make it impossible to tell."

"It's a 'he.' And those aren't bandages."

Carter turned to Mason, thinking he was making some sort of odd joke, but the look in Mason's eyes told him it was no joke. Carter felt himself go very cold and his testicles seemed to be shrinking up into his crotch as if trying to hide.

He turned back to the figure on the bed and bent his helmet close to the plastic tent. What he'd thought was a bandage was instead a thick yellow growth that covered the whole body, even the face.

"Jesus," he groaned. "What the hell *is* that? It looks like a mold . . ."

"It is."

Carter was confused. "I've seen a fair few corpses in my time but never one in a state like that. And why have you got it up here instead of in the morgue?"

"It's not a corpse." Mason's voice was bleak.

"*What!*" He stared at Mason in astonishment then back at the form on the bed. He now saw that the fluff-covered chest rose and fell perceptibly. He was glad he hadn't had time for breakfast before he'd left home.

"Yes, he's still alive," said Mason. "I suppose you could say he's one of the *lucky* ones." He made a sound that might have been a laugh. "Unlike this patient."

Mason led Carter to the adjacent bed. The naked body beneath the plastic was that of a man. Carter judged him to be in his mid-twenties. He couldn't tell for sure because from the neck up there was nothing but a lump of grey, featureless fungus. It was like a dirty cauliflower.

"Mercifully dead, but I don't dare transfer him to the morgue. The risk of contagion is too great. The man may be dead but that growth is still alive, I fear."

"But what *is* it?" demanded Carter. "Where did these people get infected with this stuff?"

"The answer to both your questions is, 'I don't know,'" said Mason. He pointed back at the first bed. "That one was picked up by the police less than two hours ago. He was spotted by the driver of a newspaper delivery van staggering along the Euston Road. The two policemen who answered the call had the good sense to bring him straight here. And this victim . . ." He indicated the body in front of them. "... was brought in by ambulance from Ladbroke Grove about an hour ago. Neighbors heard his girlfriend screaming at around 5 a.m. She was completely hysterical. She'd woken up in bed and found him like this ... beside her." Mason swallowed dryly and led Carter to the next bed.

Carter reluctantly stared through the plastic. It was almost as bad as he had feared. The body was covered with pulpy white growths. Like toadstools, the puff-ball variety.

He remembered the unusually large toadstools growing in the gutter outside the hospital and a horrible suspicion began to form in the back of his mind.

"This one's alive too," said Mason. "Staggered into the casualty department of Guy's Hospital at 4 a.m."

"It *is* some kind of fungus, isn't it," said Carter, peering at the growths.

"It looks like it. But I've tried massive doses of both nystatin and griseofulvin without any noticeable effect."

Carter nodded. Those were the two antibiotics most effective against fungal infections. "I've never seen anything like this before."

"Neither have I. I'm no expert on fungal infections but I thought I was familiar with most of the ones that can affect human beings, even the ones we don't tend to get in Britain, like histoplasmosis and coccidioidomycosis, but this ... this is outside my experience completely."

An idea occurred to Carter. "It could be some new tropical strain that a visitor from, say, Africa or India has brought in. You'd better get in touch with the Institute of Tropical Medicine, they might be able to identify this."

"I've already thought of that. My staff are making the calls now. They're also trying to contact the head of the Mycology Department at London University so that we can have stuff analysed by experts as soon as possible. But the most pressing problem—and the reason I called you—is to stop this stuff from spreading any further. This last victim was brought in from as far away as Hackney. ..." He indicated the final occupied bed.

Carter looked and saw a large, middle-aged black woman lying there. At first she seemed free of any fungal growths but then he noticed the long slits running down her limbs and torso. He looked at her face. Her eyes were open but the surface of the eyeballs was covered with a grey mold. He could see the same grey mold within the fissures in her skin. Fortunately she wasn't breathing.

"Her whole body is riddled with fungus. There's probably more of *it* than her now. One of the disturbing factors is that each of the four victims here appears to have been afflicted by a *different* type of fungus. I just don't understand it."

Carter said tonelessly, "Ladbroke Grove, Hackney, Borough . . . that's a wide area already. Have there been any more reported cases?"

"I'm afraid so. So far we've had calls from the West Middlesex Hospital, the London Hospital and the Springfield Hospital . . . they've all got cases by the sound of it."

"Springfield . . . that's Upper Tooting." The red area on Carter's mental map of London grew even bigger. "And you say it's very contagious, but exactly *how* contagious?"

"Extremely contagious," answered Mason. "The two policemen who brought in the Euston Road victim are in another ward nearby. They're both infected. The stuff is covering about twenty percent of their bodies and is spreading fast, despite all our attempts to kill it. Three ambulance men have also been stricken so far . . . and there's this."

Mason held up his right hand and opened the seals on the plastic glove. He pulled off the glove and Carter saw, on the back of Mason's hand, a patch of yellow mold.

PART TWO

THE JOURNEY

I

Flannery lurched in to Neary's, trying to ignore the pain in his bruised legs. He was positive that one of the men lined up at the bar was going to be surprised to see him and he was right. Of the several faces that turned in his direction one of them registered a fleeting look of disbelief. The face belonged to Bresnihan.

Flannery joined him at the bar.

Casually, Flannery said, "Hello, Fiach. I suppose I have you to thank for last night."

Bresnihan's attempt to look innocent was as weak as English beer. "I don't know what . . ." he began.

Flannery cut him off. "Don't waste your breath, Fiach. You might need it to explain to that poor, mistreated wife of yours why you've come home carrying your balls in a paper bag instead of in your pea-sized scrotum. I know it was you who set me up with the provos. You told them that my questions about Mulvaney had something to do with them, right?"

Bresnihan hesitated, then gave a resigned nod. "How did you get away? I figured for sure you'd be a dead man by now."

Flannery grinned. "It takes more than the IRA to stop Flannery, Fiach, my lad. You should know that."

"Oh Christ!" shouted Barry Wilson, slamming his fist onto the typewriter and making the lamp with the loose connection flicker. It was no good. Much too melodramatic. Too far over the top. None of that 'wry, sharp wit' that the reviewer in the *Irish Times* had astutely noticed in the last Flannery novel *The Meaning of Liffey*. It was more Mickey Spillane than Barry Wilson.

He frowned suddenly and cocked his head. Was that the doorbell? It was hard to tell with these damn earplugs but he'd become addicted to them as a working aid. It certainly couldn't have been the phone because he'd taken it off the hook weeks ago.

He sincerely hoped it wasn't the door bell. He didn't want a single interruption until he'd finished all the work he had to do. Apart from meeting the deadline for this fourth Flannery book—which was less than a month away—he also had to write a treatment for the proposed Flannery TV series that RTE was "semi-keen" on doing. If the TV series happened his financial problems would be over. Though the Flannery novels had been a moderate success, and their popularity was still growing, money was still in short supply. The two children, Simon and Jessica, ate up most of it and the rest was spent on paying off this damp-ridden cottage here in County Wicklow.

He heard the sound again. It was the door bell. He swore to himself and looked at his watch. It was after midnight. Who the hell would be paying him a visit all the way up here at this time of night? Couldn't be one of his neighbors. He'd made a point of alienating them all in order to ensure uninterrupted privacy.

He took out the earplugs and listened intently. The door bell rang again. This time it sounded as if someone were leaning on it. He got up and made his way out of the study and down the passage towards the front room.

Without turning on the light he crept across the floor, struggling to remember which of the boards creaked, and went to one of the front windows. Warily he peered out through a crack in the curtain . . . and got a shock.

He could see the outlines of three men outside. And all of them were carrying what looked like automatic weapons.

Alarmed, he backed away from the window. Men with guns. It could mean only one thing. The IRA. But what were they doing at his house?

At that moment there came a tremendous thump on the front door. Wilson's heart seemed to miss a beat. Christ, they were breaking down the door!

He retreated from the front room, ran down the passage and

back into his study. His mind raced as he frantically tried to think of a place to hide. There was no cellar, no attic. . . .

The front door shuddered again.

A weapon! He had to find a weapon. But what was there? He had no rifle, no shotgun . . . then he noticed the letter opener lying on his desk. He snatched it up. Not sharp, but it was long and pointed.

Then he heard the front door splintering. . . .

He turned off the study light and crawled quickly under his desk. He waited there, heart pounding like a jack hammer, clutching the letter opener.

Voices in the front room. He heard his name being called.

Shit, so it was *him* they were after. It wasn't some random attack or a case of mistaken identity. But why him? Why would the IRA be after him? Okay, so he'd poked fun at them in the Flannery books but surely he hadn't upset them enough for them to take *this* sort of action.

Maybe they intended kidnapping him. Perhaps they thought he was a rich author and figured he could raise a huge ransom. Christ, they were going to be pissed off when they found out how little he was worth.

Heavy footsteps. In the passage. Getting closer.

Hell, what could he do? What would Flannery do in a spot like this? Take the offensive, of course. Surprise them. Grab one of them, shove the letter opener against his throat and take him hostage. Then use the famous Flannery cool to talk himself out of the situation. Probably end up with them eating out of his hand; volunteering to come round and fix the door and maybe do some work in the garden as compensation.

Fuck Flannery. This was real life. Wilson shared some of Flannery's characteristics, as most authors do with their creations, but heroism, nerves of steel and a cool head in an emergency were not among them. Also Flannery was over six feet tall and built like a brick shithouse whereas Wilson was five feet ten and weighed only 160 pounds.

The footsteps got closer. The light came on. Wilson got a low angle view of three pairs of heavy black boots coming towards him across the floor.

I'll spring out, Wilson told himself, *stab one of them and then make a run for it in all the confusion.*

But he couldn't get his body to move. All he could do was crouch there helplessly. The next thing he knew there was a face peering at him only a few inches from his own. One of the men had bent down and was looking at him under the desk.

"Mr. Wilson? Mr. Barry Wilson?" inquired the face politely.

For a few seconds Wilson stared back in frozen shock. Then he managed to croak, "Yes . . . that's me." It was only then that he realized the man spoke with an English accent. "You're not Irish," he told him accusingly.

"No sir. I'm Lieutenant Smythe-Robertson of the 69th Parachute Regiment. Would you care to come out from under there, sir? We don't have much time."

Wilson crawled out from under the desk. The man helped him get to his feet. Feeling dazed, he stared round at the three of them. They were all dressed in army uniforms. "You're soldiers. *British* soldiers," he said, somewhat stupidly.

"Yessir," said the one called Smythe-Robertson. "And there's no need for *that*, sir." He looked down at Wilson's right hand.

Wilson followed his gaze and saw the letter opener. It appeared puny and ridiculous compared to the three submachine guns the soldiers were carrying. Wilson opened his hand and the letter opener fell to the floor with a clatter. "I thought you were the IRA," he muttered.

The three soldiers glanced at each other. Wilson saw something in the looks that he was not sure he liked. Resentment began to replace his numbing fear. "Look here, what the hell is going on? You come breaking into my house in the dead of night scaring the shit out of me—you'd better have a bloody good explanation. And what are you doing here in the Republic? The Irish government is going to take a pretty dim view of this, I can tell you."

Smythe-Robertson held up a hand to cut him off. "We have special dispensation, sir, due to the State of Emergency that exists in both countries. Now will you please accompany us, sir. We have a long way to travel." He gripped Wilson's arm. Wilson shook his hand away.

"State of Emergency? What State of Emergency? What the fuck are you talking about?"

"You must know what's happened on the mainland. The TV and radio's been full of it."

"I don't have a TV and I never listen to the radio when I'm up here working alone. Too distracting."

"You mean you don't know about the crisis?" Smythe-Robertson looked very surprised.

"*What* crisis?" demanded Wilson.

The soldier paused for a moment then said, "There's no time to explain it all now. We have to get moving right away."

"Moving to where?"

"Belfast."

Wilson laughed, "*I*'m not going to Belfast. I'm not going anywhere with you."

Smythe-Robertson made a gesture and his two men each grabbed one of Wilson's arms. The next thing Wilson knew he was being dragged out of his study. He tried to put up a resistance but the two soldiers didn't even seem to notice his efforts.

"You can't do this to me!" he yelled. "I'll sue you for false arrest!"

"We're not arresting you, sir," said Smythe-Robertson from close behind. "But in a State of Emergency you are obliged by law to obey our instructions. And that's what you're doing."

They dragged him out through the front doorway, stepping over the remains of the door. Wilson then received another surprise. Sitting in his front garden was a helicopter—a big one.

As the soldiers hustled him toward it, its engine roared into life and the rotor began to turn.

"Better duck, sir," yelled one of the soldiers. "We don't want to lose that valuable head of yours."

No sooner had they bundled him through a side-door in the machine than it began to rise into the air. Wilson couldn't take in what was happening. It was all too crazy to be true. If he'd put something like this in a Flannery story he'd be accused of being too far-fetched.

"Look, I can't go away anywhere! I've got a *book* to write! I've got a *deadline* to meet!" he yelled over the noise of the engine.

"Where's your publisher based, Mr. Wilson?" yelled back Smythe-Robertson.

"London, of course!"

"Mr. Wilson, there *is* no London anymore!"

2

Everything smelled of country.

Dermot Biggs breathed deeply of the warm night air and was happy. He and Sally and their three children, Sarah, Robert and Finnegan, were all thoroughly enjoying their fortnight's camping holiday. It was proving to be the success he'd hoped for but hadn't really thought possible. The usual constant bickering between the kids had stopped and the slight sexual distance he'd felt from Sally in recent months had been bridged, not once but several times.

The weather in Yorkshire had been marvelous the whole time, the car hadn't misbehaved at all, and to top it off the old farmer on whose property they were camping turned out to be the producer of a home-made beer that was one of the best things Dermot had ever tasted, as well as having the kick of Kenny Dalglish. Every time Dermot visited the farm to pick up their daily supply of eggs and fresh milk he also came away with a quart of the old man's brew.

He was carrying a quart of it now as he headed across the fields to the clump of trees beside the small river where they were camped. He was a pleasant old fellow for a farmer, Dermot reflected, though he did tend to ramble a bit at times. Like tonight when they'd been sitting in his kitchen sampling a couple of pints of a new batch. He'd been going on about something he'd heard on the radio—or *wireless*, as he called it—concerning some plague that was supposed to have broken out in London. Dermot couldn't make head nor tail of what he said and guessed he was exaggerating wildly. Pity one of the kids had dropped and broken their own radio last week, but he was sure that whatever it was could wait until they got back—perish the thought—to Liverpool the next Monday.

Besides, who gave a damn about London? When did anyone in London last give a damn about what went on north of Watford? It was practically a separate country.

Dermot's good mood persisted even when he stepped in some cow dung. He muttered, "Oh bugger," to himself and then chuckled when he switched on his flashlight to confirm that he had indeed walked into the grandfather of all cowpats. A fresh one too.

He wiped his right shoe on the grass to clean off the dung then continued to weave his tipsy way towards the camp site.

He didn't know it, and wouldn't have cared less if he did, but smears of excreta remained in the chunky patterns on the sole of his shoe. He also didn't know that the smears contained spores from the *coprophilous* fungus living in the intestine of the cow that had produced the dung.

None of this would have mattered but for the fact that the field had received an invisible shower of microscopic fungus particles carried all the way from London by the prevailing winds. The particles had first been swept very high into the sky and would have continued on over the Irish Sea if a westerly cross current hadn't caused them to be deposited onto this particular part of Yorkshire.

And as Dermot walked across the field a few of the particles were picked up by the smears of cow dung on his shoe. Each particle contained Jane Wilson's still-active enzyme, and when one of them came into contact with a *coprophilous* spore, something began to happen.

The lights were out in both the tents. Dermot had expected to find Sally still engrossed in her paperback—some epic fantasy about an adventurous leper or something. She and her silly sci-fi books, but it was because she was so hooked on the damn thing that she didn't mind him going off to get plastered with the old farmer.

He headed for the children's tent and almost tripped over a tent rope. Regaining his balance he said "*Shhhs!*" to himself and then poked his head, unsteadily, into the tent. They were all fast asleep but he kept watching them for awhile longer to make sure. They were crafty little devils.

Satisfied that they weren't faking he went to his own tent. Sally was asleep too so he undressed as quietly as he could. All went well until he tried to remove his trousers and tripped over. He flopped heavily onto Sally.

"*Wa? Uh?*" she said.

"It's only me. Sorry, possum. I'm a bit sloshed."

She muttered something he couldn't decipher and unzippered the sleeping bag a part of the way to make room for him. He crawled in, with difficulty. She was naked and felt warm. There was the slight slickness to her body that fresh perspiration gives. It felt very good, and he began to get hard.

He caressed her smooth skin and she reacted swiftly with the responses of a sexually aroused but still half-awake woman. They made love with all the pleasure of their early days together.

Later, as they slept, a thick, orange growth slowly formed outside the tent. It was looking for food, having already depleted the organic detritus in the soil.

It quickly detected the presence of a large supply of warm food nearby. Its thin hyphae, which would have been almost invisible in daylight, spread out over the ground toward the heat source. They moved swiftly, covering over 12 inches every minute. They entered the tent and spread across the grass towards the ground sheet and the end of the sleeping bag. During their love-making Dermot and his wife had emerged from the bag and were now sleeping on top of it. The tips of the hyphae touched their damp feet and began to feed on the dead outer layer of the epidermis.

As they grew further up the sleeping couple's legs the hyphae sensed a food that was more natural to the *coprophilous* fungus. They grew faster and were soon probing the warm crevices and orifices that were particularly moist and nourishing.

They entered Dermot and Sally almost simultaneously.

All the sleeping couple felt was a dim sense of increased warmth. They both relaxed into it, and their dreams were pleasant. At one point Sally became half-awake and stroked Dermot's chest. His skin seemed to have a thick, furry texture to it but she knew that was only because of the strangeness that sleep gives to the senses. It felt wonderful, she decided, as she sank back into deep sleep again.

In the other tent the children were being similarly invaded by the fungus and entering into the same peaceful state of union with it. The mutating *coprophilous* was making the necessary changes to its hosts so that it could exist in a symbiotic relationship with them without causing their destruction.

When the Biggs family awoke the next morning and saw what they had become, there was no adverse reaction—some brief moments of bewilderment but that was all. Then they began their new life, no longer needful of tents, books or clothes. From now on the fungus would take care of all their wants.

They wandered out into the meadow and got down on all fours. The grass tasted especially good at this time of the year.

3

Slocock hurt so much he knew he couldn't do another yard, let alone a lap. His legs felt like kit-bags full of suet and his throat was so raw that each breath was like swallowing a cheese grater. His heart was doing at least 180 mph and he wouldn't have been surprised if it simply packed up on him.

But he did do another lap, driving his short, stocky body on.

"Nice one, Sarge!" shouted young Feely who was sitting on one of the low benches that ringed the track. There was someone with him but Slocock, his eyes stinging with sweat, couldn't make out who it was.

Slocock staggered off the track and collapsed onto the grass. He lay there on his back, chest heaving. The hot midday sun beat down on him and he screwed his eyes shut against it.

In the distance there was a distinctive *crump* sound. The bastards were at it again. A big one too. Possibly another car bomb. Despite what had happened on the mainland, and what was *still* happening, the bloody IRA had stepped up their campaign against the army. *They can't drive us out now*, thought Slocock bitterly, *don't they realize there's no place left for us to go?*

"You want to be careful, Sarge. Especially at your age," came Feely's voice from close by. Slocock smiled to himself. Feely was a good kid.

"If someone had said that to your old man," wheezed Slocock, "you'd be nothing but a dried-up puddle in an old rubber lying in some Liverpool alley. And what a loss to the world that would have been."

Feely laughed. Some people—well, a *lot* of people—couldn't take Slocock. And Slocock had convinced himself he liked it that way, particularly since Marge. But Feely refused to be offended by anything Slocock said and usually gave as good as he got. This time, however, all he said was, "You've got a visitor, Sarge." And his voice held a note of amusement in it.

Slocock opened his eyes. Sweat continued to blur his vision and he could only distinguish two vague forms outlined against the sun.

"Good afternoon, sergeant," said a female voice. A very nice female voice.

Slocock wiped his eyes with the back of his hand and squinted. He could now make out a woman in her late twenties. She was strikingly attractive. She had large eyes, high cheek bones, and a wide, suggestive mouth. Her hair was short and very black. And though she was wearing a pair of baggy jeans and a shapeless khaki shirt he could tell her body was lean and muscular. She held herself well.

"Begorrah, Feely," he said in a mock Irish accent, "you've brought your dear old grannie to see your beloved Sarge."

"I'm Kimberley Fairchild. *Doctor* Kimberley Fairchild. I'd say it's a pleasure to meet you, Sargeant Slocock, but I've already been warned about you."

"Lies. Filthy lies spread about by my envious inferiors. I am in reality the pasteurized milk of human kindness. So what can I do you for, Doctor?"

"Nothing in particular. I just wanted to take a look at you."

He spread his arms. "Look all you want. Feast your eyes. It will mean reappraising your ideal of male beauty but that's the price you must pay for the privilege."

She laughed. "All I see is a short, overweight, and out of condition man in his mid-thirties who has a tendency to freckle and who shouldn't be lying out in this sun with that sort of skin."

Feely laughed too. "She's right, Sarge. You're starting to look like a burned tomato."

"That's indignation, lad, not sunburn," he growled. To Kimberley Fairchild he said, "If I'm such a disappointing specimen, Doctor, why are you wasting your time looking at me?"

"Curiosity, Sergeant. I wanted to see who I was going to be traveling with."

Slocock's body twitched. Then he abruptly sat up and stared at her. "*You're* coming too? For fuck's sake *why*?"

"You don't have to sound so pleased," she said dryly.

"But Christ, don't you know what we have to *do* over there? What lame-brained arse-hole came up with the idea of including *you* in the operation? I'm going to have enough to worry about without playing nursemaid for you."

"Oh, stuff the macho drivel, Sergeant. You've got it back-to-front. I'm to be *your* nursemaid. I'm a doctor, remember, and you're going to need one over there."

"Hah! What good will a doctor be? You've all been pretty useless so far. About the only thing you can do is hand out the death pills when . . ."

He didn't finish but glanced instead at the burned-out patch in the center of the grass area. That was where Hibbert had been incinerated. He'd managed to stagger this far before they'd caught up with him and surrounded him. Then they'd let loose with the three flame-throwers at once. But it was amazing how long he'd kept screaming.

"Believe me, Sergeant, you'll be glad I'm along. And don't worry, I *can* take care of myself. I grew up with firearms. I'm a crack shot."

It took an effort to tear his gaze away from the blackened patch of ground. He looked at her more closely, noting the touch of arrogance in her eyes; her air of total self-confidence. She was definitely something out of the ordinary. She *had* to be. No one in her right mind would volunteer to go where they were going. He knew what *his* reasons were. He wondered about hers.

Unexpectedly she gave him a dazzling smile and said, "Come on, Sergeant. I'll buy you and the Corporal here a drink. That is if you're allowed to drink at this time of the day."

"We're both off-duty. A drink would be fine." He struggled to his feet like an old man carrying two sacks of potatoes. Feely knew better than to lend a hand.

As usual, the bar was packed when they arrived. It stayed open 24 hours a day now as there were always plenty of off-duty men to fill it. The number of soldiers in the base had quadrupled since the Emergency. It was the same at every base in Northern Ireland.

Their entrance caused a stir. Everyone looked in their direction and there were wolf-whistles and crude jeers. It wouldn't have been like this a few weeks ago, Slocock reflected. Oh yes, these brainless bums would have reacted the same way to a woman like Kimberley Fairchild walking into their private male preserve, but not in so *blatant* a way. Things are beginning to crumble, he realized. The discipline is giving way. With the center gone the rest of the structure, what there is left of it, is collapsing. . . .

"I think you'd be more comfortable in the Officer's Club," he told her.

"Nonsense, Sergeant," she said and plunged into the crowd toward the bar. Slocock watched her walk coolly through the offensive rabble, then followed after her with Feely bringing up the rear. He ignored the jibes along the way. He'd long since given up worrying about his pride. Marge had taken care of that. As everyone back at Aldershot had known about her sleeping around months before she had walked out on him he knew he was looked upon as being not much of a man. Unusually, for such a situation, Marge had got all the sympathy. No one blamed her for having affairs, because he was generally regarded as a bastard. Many just thought she was trying to get away from him but the truth was even more humiliating than the worst of the gossip he'd picked up about himself—she *had* been trying to rub his nose in the fact that he could no longer even begin to satisfy her. And when her 'affairs' entered double figures he gave up counting.

He pushed ahead of Kimberley and cleared a space for her at the bar. He had no difficulty in intimidating the men there—they may have despised him, but they still feared him. And for good reason.

"What'll you have?" he asked her.

"What do grannies normally drink?" she asked.

"My granny drank brandy."

"Then I'll have a brandy."

"It killed her."

"Then I'll have a double."

Slocock grinned, ordered her drink, a pint of bitter for Feely and a double scotch for himself.

While waiting for the drinks he turned to Feely. "How did last night's mission south of the border go?"

"Okay. No real fuss except we had to practically drag the bloke out from under his desk. He was hiding there. Thought we were the bloody IRA." Feely laughed. "Bit of a wimp if you ask me. Beats me why we had to go fetch him. You any idea, Sarge?"

Slocock grimaced. "Yeah. Too many." He glanced at Kimberley. "You met him yet?"

She shook her head. "No, but I will soon." She looked at her watch. "In just over an hour's time. At a briefing. You'll be attending it as well, I gather."

"Wouldn't miss it for the world," he said sourly. "I hear they're going to show us some great snuff movies."

"I understand you had something like that right here in the base. A man called Hibbert . . . ?"

Slocock downed his scotch with one swallow and gestured to the barman for a refill. "Yeah. Percy Hibbert. He came in the last batch to be evacuated from Holyhead before they slammed the doors. Spent two days having every inch of his body checked for any sign of the stuff like everybody else and finally got a clean bill of health. Was here for a whole four days before it happened."

Slocock's second drink arrived. He grabbed it thankfully. He swallowed half, then continued. "On the morning of the fourth day he'd been here I was walking by the shower blocks and heard a bigger commotion in there than usual. I go for a look-see and almost get knocked down by a stampede of naked guys. Then through the steam comes Hibbert, screaming for help. He was bare-arsed too and I could see his whole body was starting to split open with this green and black stuff pushing itself out of him. He came right up to me and *grabbed* me." Slocock shuddered at the memory and finished his second double.

"I shoved him away. He goes sprawling across the floor but gets up and runs off. I start screaming for someone to go fetch the bloody flame-throwers and then follow him. We chased him around the camp for nearly a quarter of an hour. We finally cornered him on the football field—out where we were just now."

"And that was five days ago?"

Slocock nodded. He was watching, yet again, Hibbert's blackened body writhing and kicking as the three jets of fire sprayed over him.

"It's fortunate there's been no other outbreak since then," said Kimberley. "You were all very lucky."

Feely said, "The whole place still stinks of disinfectant. And everything Hibbert touched was burned. We even burned down the shower block. But since then everyone's been as nervous as hell. Most of the lads spend every spare minute checking themselves for a sign of the stuff."

"Or checking each other. The faggots are over the moon," growled Slocock. He was still embarrassed at the state of panic he'd been in for 24 hours after the Hibbert incident. He'd torn off all his clothes and locked himself in a bathroom in the officers' block. He'd sat in an empty bathtub, shaking uncontrollably, and poured a bottle of disinfectant over himself.

"It's unusual the fungus took so long to make itself evident in this man Hibbert," said Kimberley reflectively. "It must have been a variety that incubates in the blood. Possibly the heat and humidity in the shower room caused it to suddenly grow."

Slocock scowled at her. She could have been discussing the weather. "Just who *are* you, Dr. Kimberley Fairchild, and what are you doing here? You're not British, I know that." He had detected an underlying accent beneath her semi-posh English one.

"The Sergeant has sharp ears," she said with a slightly mocking smile. "You're right, I'm not English, though usually most people presume I am. I was educated there but I was born in South Africa. My parents had a farm there. Near Kimberley, of course."

Slocock nodded. That explained her remark about growing up with firearms. "So how come you're here in Northern Ireland?"

"I flew over from Paris, which is where I live these days. My field is tropical medicine. I've worked in countries like Angola, Zaire, and Mozambique and I'm an expert on all the tropical diseases, including the African fungal diseases, of which there are several. As soon as I heard what was happening I called and offered my services to your government-in-exile. As most of their own experts are trapped on the mainland, they accepted my offer."

"Okay. I'm with you so far. You're a good Samaritan. But why have you volunteered to go on this mission? Surely you're more use to the authorities here. You must know the chances of us coming back are pretty remote."

"Let's just say I have my. . . ."

She didn't get to the end of the sentence. A soldier had suddenly lurched up to the bar and put his arm around her. "Hullo, darling, what are you doing with these faggots? Why don't you come and drink with some real men?" he said in a loud, slurred voice.

Slocock had been expecting something like this. Out of the corner of his eye he'd seen the bunch at the nearby table nudging each other and pointing at Kimberley. They'd obviously been egging each other on to make a move—and now one of their number had. It was Baxter. He was a six foot four inch pile of balding flab. And as drunk as an Irish priest. Slocock knew he wouldn't have had the guts to do what he was doing if he was even half-sober.

Without saying anything Slocock stepped quickly in front of Baxter and hit him hard at a point midway between his navel and his crotch.

Baxter let go of Kimberley and started to double over. As he did so Slocock head-butted him in the face. Baxter toppled backwards and hit the floor with a crash that made the glasses behind the bar rattle.

The place went quiet. Slocock turned his back on Baxter and his companions, confident that no one else would try it with him. And anyway, Feely would warn him if they did.

Feely said admiringly, "Neat job, Sarge. One of your better efforts."

"Thank you, Feely."

"If *I'm* supposed to be impressed by that you've made a big mistake," said Kimberley who had maintained her cool poise throughout the incident. "I find that sort of thing a turn-off. I was quite capable of handling the situation *my* way. There was no need for juvenile violence."

"Doctor, I didn't do that for you, believe me," Slocock said as he gestured at the barman for another round. "I did it for me."

He turned to her. "Hasn't anyone told you yet why I'm needed on that mission? We both know why Wilson has to go, and according to you your medical skills are going to be essential for keeping him alive long enough to do the job, but what about me?"

Stiffly she said, "I was told you were a good soldier."

He choked on his scotch. Feely guffawed.

When Slocock stopped coughing he said, "The brass told you that? Jesus! Look, lady, I'm being sent because I'm *not* a good soldier. I'm only good at one thing and that's damaging people. Trouble is, once I start I find it hard to stop, and the army finds that kind of embarrassing, especially over here. I'm a liability to them. They're happy to get rid of me." He drank the rest of his scotch.

"You're going to make yourself drunk," said Kimberley accusingly.

"Lady, I hoped to be smashed out of my brain by the time I have to see those videos they're going to show us. I advise you to be the same."

4

Barry Wilson was furious.

It had been several hours since he'd been bundled into the helicopter but still no one had explained to him the reason behind his compulsory visit to Belfast. Of course he could only take their word for it that he *was* in Belfast. It had still been dark when they touched down and all he'd seen were a few drab, military-looking buildings around the landing area.

Now he was sitting alone in an almost bare room that smelled strongly of disinfectant. There were a few hard-backed chairs scattered around, one of which he was sitting on, and a table covered in a green felt cloth. Behind it there was a blackboard and a large map of the British Isles. It was like being in a seedy school room.

Wilson jumped as the door opened behind him. He looked round and saw two officers enter the room. One was a little older than him, probably 36 or 37, the other in late middle age. He was relieved to see they were just carrying clipboards and didn't appear to be armed.

"Hello Mr. Wilson," said the older one. "Sorry to keep you waiting but you can imagine how things are here at the moment." They sat down at the table and stared at him. There was curiosity and expectancy in their gaze, and also a touch of desperation. Wilson saw that the younger man, who sat very stiffly, looked particularly anxious. He also had a tic in his right cheek.

Wilson said, "It's *Doctor*, not Mister. And no, I can't imagine how things are here at the moment. All I know is that I was kidnapped at gunpoint. My house was broken into and is probably still open to looters, children and cats pissing over the family heirlooms. I want an apology, an explanation, compensation and a quick trip home. Not necessarily in that order."

The older officer sighed. Then, "First let us introduce ourselves. My name is Major Peterson. This is Captain O'Connell." The thin-featured younger officer gave Wilson a curt nod. The Major continued, "I understand from Lieutenant Smythe-Robertson that you claim you are unaware of recent events?" He obviously found this difficult to believe.

"That's right, and I'm *still* unaware of recent events, whatever they may be. I kept asking your Lieutenant Smith what the hell was going on but he didn't tell me anything apart from a bad-taste joke about London."

O'Connell leaned forward, his pale, sharp face looking even more haggard than earlier. "You really don't know what's going on over there?"

Wilson shook his head with annoyance. "For the hundredth time, *no* I don't."

"What in God's name have you been doing for the past two weeks?" demanded Peterson.

"I've been alone in my cottage writing. As you must know I'm a writer. I write the Flannery books." He paused very briefly for the signs of recognition every writer hopes for but very rarely receives. Here he got none at all. "Flannery is an Irish private detective," he explained sulkily.

"For two weeks!" It sounded to Wilson as though the Major's astonishment was more to do with the length of time that anyone in his right mind would spend writing than at the self-imposed solitude.

"It actually takes a little longer than that to write a book," said Wilson. "I was racing to finish it off after a visit from my children. I can't do any work at all when they're around. I need total isolation and no interruptions. It's the way I work—in concentrated bursts."

"No newspapers? No television?" asked Peterson.

"No."

"What about phone calls? Visits from your neighbors?"

"I took the phone off the hook and my neighbors and I don't speak to each other as a rule."

"Extraordinary," murmured Peterson.

"And now can you tell me what all the panic's about? I presume it's not World War III, otherwise we'd all be glowing in the dark by now."

"No, it's not World War III, Dr. Wilson," said Peterson. "But before I explain there are some questions I must ask you." He glanced at his clipboard. "You *are* married to Dr. Jane Wilson, are you not?"

Wilson was taken aback by the introduction of his estranged wife into this bizarre conversation. "Yes," he said. "Why?"

Peterson ignored his question. "And she was a mycologist working at the Institute of Tropical Biology in London?"

Wilson didn't care for his use of the word "was." He began to get a queasy sensation in the pit of his stomach. "That officer *was* joking, wasn't he? When he said that London no longer existed?"

Peterson and O'Connell exchanged a look. The younger officer's face was now completely white. Wilson's anxiety increased. Something *had* happened in London. Something horrendous. But if it wasn't a nuclear war what was it? Some sort of nuclear accident? Or had we dropped one of our own H-Bombs on it by mistake? It was probably the Americans' fault—they were always having accidents with their bloody bombs and missiles, dropping them all over the place. "Broken Arrows" they called them.

"Look, you've got to tell me!" he demanded. "My children are in London."

Peterson held up a hand. "The officer was exaggerating. London still exists. It's just that . . . well, it's been *changed*."

O'Connell suddenly bent forward and put his hands over his mouth. His shoulders began to shake and he made a dry retching sound. Wilson didn't know if he was crying or about to throw up.

Major Peterson regarded O'Connell with a pained expression. "Perhaps you should leave, Captain. I can handle this."

With a visible effort O'Connell straightened and regained his composure. He wiped his mouth with the back of his hand and took a deep breath. "I'm fine, sir. Really. I'll be all right."

Peterson turned back to Wilson. "About your wife," he began.

Wilson cut him short. "Why the hell do you keep going on about Jane? One moment we're talking about some disaster that's befallen London and the next you're back asking questions about my wife! What's she got to do with any of this?"

"Believe me, Dr. Wilson," said Peterson, "she has a lot to do with it. Now please let me continue with my questions. I assure you they are all relevant to the situation which I will explain to you shortly."

Wilson sighed impatiently. It was like something out of Kafka. "Go on," he said.

"Your wife is regarded as one of the top experts in the field of mycology, correct?"

"Yes. Whenever and wherever in the world people get together to discuss fungi my wife's name is invariably mentioned in tones of awe. What of it?"

"And you're a mycologist too, I understand?"

"I *used* to be," Wilson corrected him. "I decided I'd made what is called a career error. I gave it all up to become a writer. Besides, one scientific genius in the family is enough." He couldn't keep the trace of bitterness out of his voice.

"But you kept in touch with what your wife was doing?" asked Peterson. "In her research, I mean."

Wilson nodded. "Couldn't avoid it. All she ever talks about."

"And what was she doing?"

"Trying to breed a new species of mushroom. Big mushrooms that would grow quickly and be about ten times richer in protein than the ordinary sort. She has visions of solving the world food shortage with the things. Never thinks small, my wife."

"Do you know the *exact* method she was using to create these big mushrooms?" asked O'Connell eagerly.

Wilson frowned. "Well, I don't know the exact details of her current line of research. I'm not that interested anymore so I haven't bothered to ask. But I know she's been tinkering about with the chemical structure of the mushroom enzymes."

The two officers exchanged another glance. Then Peterson wrote something down on his clipboard. "That's a start anyway," he said.

Increasingly puzzled, Wilson said, "Look, you're talking as if she actually succeeded with these mushrooms. Has she?"

"Oh, she's succeeded all right," said Peterson dryly. "And she may indeed solve the world food problem, but not in the way she envisaged."

"Will you *please* tell me what you're talking about?!" demanded Wilson.

O'Connell gestured at the map of Britain on the wall. "Dr. Wilson, most of southern England, as well as other areas of the mainland, is infested with fungi. The stuff is growing on everything, including people. Millions have died already. And they're the lucky ones." His voice dried up and he shook his head helplessly, unable to continue.

Wilson stared at him, then at Peterson. The expression in their eyes told him it was no joke. His mind reeled as the enormity of O'Connell's words sank in. "But . . ." he began, and stopped. He couldn't think of anything to say. Finally all he managed was a lame, "It's incredible."

"It certainly is," agreed Peterson. "When it started it was as if the world had gone mad. No one could explain what was happening. The fungus just began sprouting all over the place for no apparent reason. Then the boffins came up with a theory. Something was reacting with all the different species of fungi it came in contact with, causing them to grow and mutate at a tremendous speed. You're the expert, Dr. Wilson. Just how many species of fungi are there?"

In a daze, Wilson said, "Nobody knows for sure. The fungal kingdom is a huge one. There are probably over 100,000 recognized species and a lot we haven't discovered yet. They range from microscopic fungi, molds, lichens, and yeasts to fungi like toadstools, puff-balls, and stinkhorns . . ."

"Well *every* single species of fungi within the affected area is going berserk," said Peterson. "And the area of contagion is expanding very fast. It's predicted it will cover all of England, Scotland and Wales within two months."

"Jesus," whispered Wilson. "My kids . . . what about London?"

"I'll be blunt, Dr. Wilson. Things are bad there. Very bad. That's where the plague began. The city is now cut off completely from the outside world. We have no communication with anyone in it. Apparently one type of fungus has developed a taste for electronics. All the phone, radio, and telecommunications equipment in London has rotted away, along with a lot of other materials. Anyway it's doubtful if anyone in London is still capable of rational conversation now—the last radio transmissions from the place were pure gibberish."

Wilson was thinking of Simon and Jessica and kicking himself that he hadn't let them stay on longer in Ireland as they'd wanted to. No, he'd sent them packing back to Jane's parents in Highgate so he could get back to work on his bloody book! Christ, had his damn selfishness sent them to their deaths? *No!* He couldn't let himself believe that. They had to be still alive. Surely not everyone in London had been affected? With difficulty he forced his attention back to what Peterson had just said. "Gibberish? What do you mean? What exactly *is* the situation in London?"

O'Connell answered, "The fungus affects its victims in different ways. Some species simply kill people—they grow all over them and riddle their bodies with their roots . . ."

"Hyphae," corrected Wilson automatically.

O'Connell glared at him and continued. "The victims are literally eaten away. And some are killed from within. The fungi grows inside their bodies and then breaks out."

"We had a case of that right here on the base," said Peterson. He grimaced. "Horrible business."

"But there's one species of fungus, or perhaps more than one, that doesn't kill its victim," O'Connell went on. "Or at least not right away. It acts like a kind of parasite. It feeds on its victims but at the same time it keeps them alive."

"You mean a symbiotic relationship develops?" asked Wilson, the scientist in him becoming intrigued in spite of himself. "How exactly?"

"The fungus *changes* its victim in some way. Metabolically. So that they're no longer . . . human. They end up not minding the ghastly stuff growing on them, *in* them." His voice dried up again and he stared into space.

"You'll have to excuse Captain O'Connell," said Peterson uneasily. "He, uh, lost his wife that way."

"I shot her," said O'Connell in a dead voice. "I had to." Suddenly he leaped to his feet and pointed an accusing finger at Wilson. "And it's *your* bloody wife who's the cause of all this!" he shouted. "*Your* fucking woman with her fucking experiments!"

"Take it easy, Captain," said Peterson, grabbing him by the arm. "Calm down, just calm down. I know it's difficult for you but it's difficult for all of us."

The anger faded from O'Connell's face, leaving a blank void that was even more disturbing to Wilson. He sat slowly down again, like a puppet being lowered on strings.

Wilson said desperately, "How do you know that Jane had anything to do with this? Why can't it be the result of some natural phenomenon?"

"You're a scientist, Dr. Wilson," said Peterson. "Can you think of any natural reason why every species of fungus should suddenly behave in this way?"

Wilson had to admit he couldn't. "But I don't see why it's necessarily linked with my wife's research."

"Your wife's laboratory was pin-pointed as the source of the infection by an investigator with the Public Health Department, a Dr. Bruce Carter. He did a heroic job. He kept his investigation going even after conditions became totally chaotic in London—and after he'd contracted a fungus infection himself. He got a radio message out four days ago, shortly before all communication with London ceased. He was absolutely positive about his findings." Peterson leaned forward and stared hard at Wilson. "Some sort of genetically engineered organism had been let loose in the environment. And that something had come from *your* wife's laboratory."

Wilson felt a terrible sense of despair settle over him. He gave a deep sigh. "What exactly got out?"

"We don't know yet," answered Peterson. "The boffins have been analyzing samples of the fungi ever since the outbreak began, but they haven't been able to isolate the agent responsible for the mutations. I've been told it's like trying to find the proverbial needle in the haystack. Your information that your wife was working in the area of enzymes should narrow down the hunt, but it's still possible they won't isolate the cause before the stuff spreads across all of England . . . and beyond."

Wilson frowned. "But surely—if Jane really is responsible—all you have to do is send someone to her lab to get her notes and records. They would tell you everything you needed to know."

"We tried that. Three days ago. A group of volunteers flew by helicopter into London. Wearing anti-contamination gear they were winched down onto the roof of the Institute of Tropical Biology. They located your wife's lab but it had been stripped clean of all its records."

"But who would have . . . ?" Wilson began.

"Who else but your wife?" said O'Connell coldly. "No one else knew."

"That doesn't sound like anything Jane would do," Wilson protested. "If she realized what had happened she would have told the authorities everything they needed to know about her work. She wouldn't have tried to conceal what she'd done."

"Who knows her current state of mind?" said Peterson with a shrug. "The knowledge that she is responsible for such a massive catastrophe may have proved too much for her. Or—and I'm sorry to have to say this—she may have fallen victim to one of the symbiotic fungi."

Wilson winced. "What about her home? Has anyone checked that?"

"Yes. The search team flew there from the Institute. They reported no sign of either your wife or her papers. Soon afterward they were attacked by a mob. The helicopter crew lost all contact and had to return without them."

"Jesus," muttered Wilson and wiped the sweat from his forehead with the back of his hand. It had become hot and stuffy in the bleak room. "What kind of mob?"

"We don't know. Possibly consisting of people driven mad by their fungal infections, but we can't be sure."

Wilson was silent. It seemed incredible that London had been transformed into some kind of nightmare world in such a short space of time.

Peterson cleared his throat uncomfortably and said, "So that's why we need you."

"Need me?" he asked, startled. "Why?"

"We want you to go to London, Dr. Wilson. We want you to find your wife, if she's still alive. If she's not we want you to locate her notes."

Wilson stared at him in horror. "Go to London? After what you've been telling me? No way."

"Dr. Wilson, no one knows your wife better than you do. You have the best chance of all of finding her. You're also a mycologist—you'll know what to look for among her notes. You are, I'm afraid, indispensable to this mission. And pray you're successful. We are under increasing pressure from other countries—France in particular—to authorize the use of nuclear weapons on the mainland. They want H-Bombs dropped not only on the affected areas but on every part of England, Scotland and Wales to stop the fungus completely."

"I don't care! I'm not going and that's final!" cried Wilson.

Contemptuously O'Connell said, "You don't understand, Doctor, you have no choice in the matter. The Acting Prime Minister has already decided you *are* going." He glanced at his watch. "In less than eight hours, as a matter of fact."

5

Ilya Nechvolodov glanced at his co-pilot Terenty who was dozing fitfully. Every now and then Terenty would jerk awake, glance in momentary panic at the control panels of the TU 144, then grin sheepishly at Ilya. Within seconds his eyelids would slip down again and a faint but irritating snore would bubble up from the back of his mouth.

As usual, Ilya reflected with annoyance, the younger pilot had been overdoing his night life again. The myth of supersonic aircraft pilots being romantic, devil-may-care, sexual supermen had instilled itself too deeply into Terenty's brain. From what Ilya had heard he was trying to prove it with every woman under 30 in Moscow but the effects of all these sexual marathons on Terenty's concentration was seriously worrying Ilya.

He'd tried speaking to Terenty about it, warning him that he was putting his career, and all its accompanying privileges, at risk but he wouldn't listen. Had the TU 144 not been carrying an important, if junior, Soviet fisheries official to a conference in Iceland he might have risked creating a fake emergency involving some simulated turbulence to give Terenty a beneficial jolt. As it was he would have no choice but to report him when they returned to Moscow. Terenty was a friend, true, but Ilya could not afford to put his own career at risk because of him. There was Alina to think of. She would leave him at once if they lost their five room apartment.

As the Russian version of the Concorde flew far to the north of Britain it passed through an area where high altitude winds were saturated with minor detritus that had been dragged up from the earth's surface in a series of stages by means of gusts and updrafts. Anything smaller than a speck of dust was trapped there forever. Bacteria, microscopic seeds, and, of course, fungal spores and fragments of the thread-like hyphae that make up a fungus.

A few, a very few, of the latter contained the Jane Wilson

enzyme. But it only took one to produce the subsequent disaster. . . .

The cone of turbulence created by the passing of the TU 144 swept this particular particle near the superstructure of the aircraft. There, by chance, it entered one of the ventilation ducts that aerated the fuel tanks.

The tank it had entered was part of a system transferring fuel around the plane in order to maintain the aircraft's trim during flight. The tanks and their fuel had another purpose too, apart from feeding the hungry engines; the vast quantities of liquid were used to dissipate the friction-created heat from the surface of the fuselage.

In the partially-filled tanks the temperature was high but in those that remained full it generally never rose above about 40 degrees centigrade. At that temperature a certain fungus called *aspergillus fumigatus*—more generally known for giving chickens lung infections—found an ideal environment in the aviation fuel. Many fungi grew, small but persistent, in the tanks during each flight. Between flights they were scoured out, but during flights a series of filters in the fuel system prevented them from getting where they might cause damage.

The system had always worked, until now . . .

When Jane Wilson's super-enzyme came into contact with the *aspergillus* it began the process of altering the genetic code within the fungus. The mutating cells spread out and altered others. Very quickly all the *aspergillus* fungi within the tank had changed.

They began to exploit the tremendous food potential of the fuel. They broke it down and used it to grow. When all the fuel in that tank had been exhausted it sent hyphae out across the tank's surface until it located a way out. The strands thickened and began to probe through the pipes that connected the tanks until they found more food. As the fungus grew it started to block the movement of fuel. This caused the aircraft's computer to try and reroute the dwindling supply that was still accessible through different pipes, but it soon ran out of alternatives.

It was at this point that Ilya became aware of what was happening.

The instrument display screen in front of him, which had been showing simulations of the airspeed indicator, the altimeter, the horizontal situation indicator, and the attitude director, suddenly displayed just a single simulation of the fuel flow indicator. It was outlined with a flashing red square and a loud buzzing sound filled the flight deck.

A jolt of alarm shook Ilya and he saw that the flow from the tanks was nil. And yet a glance showed him that the tanks still held plenty of fuel according to the fuel capacity indicator. That meant a blockage of some kind. But surely not in *all* of the flow pipes . . . ?

At that moment there was silence as the Tupolev TU 144's powerful Kuznetzov engines abruptly cut out. One second the afterburning turbofan engines were providing 44,000 pounds of thrust; the next they were nothing but dead weight.

As Ilya frantically tried to think of what to do Terenty stirred and said, "Hey, what's the matter?"

Ignoring him Ilya reached for the auxiliary fuel tank switch. The auxiliary tank should have been cut in automatically by the computer but he guessed that because the computer still registered the other tanks as full it saw no reason to do so.

He threw the switch but nothing happened.

"Ilya, what the fuck is happening?" cried Terenty, staring at the display screens. "Why have we lost power?"

The TU 144 was rapidly losing air speed. Ilya knew, as he pulled back on the elevons controls to keep the nose as high as possible, that it wouldn't be long before their glide turned into a dive.

The engines roared back into life. The fuel from the auxiliary tank, which was not connected to the trimming system, had finally reached them.

Ilya gave a sigh of relief and turned to Terenty. He spoke quickly and calmly, "Fuel blockage. But a simultaneous one in all the pipes—which makes me think it's a computer malfunction. Remember that American 747 a couple of years back that almost crashed when its computer simply switched off its fuel supply?"

Terenty nodded, his face gray with shock. "What can we do?"

"We must override the computer. There's not sufficient fuel in the auxiliary to get us to Reykjavik." He glanced at his chart. "We could just make it to Scotland, but that's off-limits because of the quarantine."

"What if it's a real blockage?" asked Terenty.

"Pray that it's not."

The flight deck door opened and Yaroslav entered. Yaroslav was the flight engineer and had been taking his break in the main cabin, socializing with the VIP passenger and his entourage.

"What the fuck are you doing up here?" he cried angrily. "You scared the shit out of our passengers just then." He didn't need to add that he had been equally scared. His face said everything.

Ilya explained as he swiftly threw a series of switches that would cut out the main computer and transfer control of the aircraft to one of the three emergency back-up computers. His hope was that this would cancel the bug in the main one that had shut off the fuel.

The *aspergillus* fungus, meanwhile, had exhausted the fuel in the tanks and was spreading its hyphae out to search for more food. Continuing to mutate, the fungi forced its hyphae into the microscopic fissures within the aluminum skin of the tanks, having already consumed the lining of rubber sealant.

The rear fuel tank, positioned below the tail, was the first to rupture. The fungus continued to expand, penetrating the hydraulic and air systems. The rich supply of much-needed oxygen in the latter caused it to grow even faster. Shortly afterwards it entered the main cabin via several air ducts toward the rear. Here it found a rich source of carbohydrates and water.

Nina Tsvigun, one of the stewardesses, was in the process of calming down the passengers in her section of the cabin. The flare-up of panic that had occurred when the engines had cut out seemed to be over, but then suddenly she heard screams from the very rear of the plane.

She hurried along the aisle and then came to a dead stop, unable to believe what she was seeing. From the punkah louvers above the seats something that looked like thick borscht was oozing into the cabin at a very fast rate. Several passengers were already covered with the thick, ropy strands. They were struggling to break free but couldn't seem to get the stuff off them. One man, whose head was entirely enveloped, stopped struggling even as she watched and slumped in his seat. His jacket then began to cave inwards as if he were being deflated like an inner tube.

She didn't wait to see anything else. She turned and ran.

Ilya cursed. He had tried two of the back-up computers but still couldn't get the fuel flowing again. Only one computer left to try.

"Keep the damn nose up, can't you!" he yelled at Terenty who had taken over control of the elevons.

"It's not me!" cried Terenty. "We're losing power. Look!"

Ilya looked and saw that the fuel flow indicator was flashing red on the display screen again. It meant that the auxiliary fuel was now being blocked off as well. But *why*? If it wasn't a computer malfunction, what was the cause?

The flight deck door opened again. It was Nina. "There's something getting into the cabin!" she cried, her voice cracking with hysteria. "It's dropping on the passengers . . . and it moves as if it's alive!"

"Have you lost your mind, Nina!" Ilya exploded angrily. But then he heard the screams coming from the main cabin and knew that *something* very bad was happening back there.

"Yaroslav! Terenty! Go and see what the problem is!" he ordered, not taking his eyes away from the console.

The two men hurried from the flight deck, followed by Nina. Ilya continued to run through every emergency procedure he could think of, but nothing worked. Then the engines cut out again.

"Damn," he whispered as he sat there seething in helpless frustration. He couldn't die like this, not knowing *why* he was dying. If he'd made some stupid flying error or the wings had fallen off, then yes, that would be understandable but this . . .

It was only then, in the silence caused by the lack of power, that he became aware the screaming had stopped in the main cabin.

Then he heard the door slowly open behind him.

"Terenty? Yaroslav?" he said, still not looking round.

There was no answer. But a strange odor filled the cabin. And then he felt a warm soft sensation on the back of his neck, like a woman's kiss.

He started to turn but the mutated *aspergillus* fungus engulfed him before he even had a chance to see what was happening.

As Ilya died in suffocating blackness his last thoughts were of his five-room apartment. He wondered who would get it.

Devoid of human life, the Tupelov TU 144 flew on silently for a time. Then its nose dipped lower and lower and it began a shallow, gliding dive that would end in the Norwegian Sea 50,000 feet below.

6

The tape wasn't started until Slocock and Kimberley had slipped, rather noisily, into their seats. Slocock saw that Peterson was giving him a particularly dirty look. Stuff him, thought Slocock. He needs me too much to give me a hard time. Let him try and find another volunteer for the crazy mission at this late stage.

There were two other people in the small room. One was Captain O'Connell, who looked as if he was close to unravelling his entire ball of twine, and a man in his early thirties who Slocock didn't recognize. He presumed he was the writer, Wilson, who was supposed to be the star of the mission. Slocock wasn't impressed. Wilson was sucking on a cigarette as if it was a nipple and looking almost as unravelled as O'Connell. Slocock decided he was going to be as much use on the mainland as a devout virgin at an orgy.

Slocock switched his attention to the screen when the familiar theme music from the BBC's nine o'clock news program began.

"This is four days after the outbreak was first detected," said Peterson over the soundtrack.

Slocock watched with interest. He hadn't seen any of the news programs during the first week of the plague—he never watched much TV—and by the time he'd been inclined to see what was going on all transmissions from the mainland had been stopped.

A news reader had appeared on the screen and was saying, "There have been tens of thousands more cases reported today of the fungal infections that have been plaguing the capital since last Tuesday—a crisis that is already being described as potentially the worst threat to face mankind since the Black Death in the Middle Ages . . .

"Although the cause of the outbreak is still unknown, work is continuing at government and private research laboratories throughout the country to find a way to curb the spread of the killer disease. A government spokesman has just announced that a breakthrough is expected at any moment. In the meantime the government advises everyone in the London area to stay at home, avoid contact with other people, and await further instructions. A strict quarantine line has been imposed around the city as a precautionary measure and movement across it is strictly forbidden.

"But as these aerial pictures show, many people have been trying to get out of London, resulting in confrontation with armed police and soldiers . . ."

An overhead shot of a major roadway appeared on the screen. It was jammed with vehicles and people. A different voice took over on the soundtrack: "John Lurton, BBC News speaking . . . I'm in a helicopter above London's North Circular road where it forms a junction with Green Lane. The ring road around London is being used as the quarantine boundary line. Troops and police all along the ring road have effectively sealed off the city but people are continually trying to get through. Below you can see a stream of cars and pedestrians moving north along Green Lane toward the barrier at the junction."

The camera zoomed in on the crowd. Men, women, and children were packed into a tight snake of humanity moving relentlessly forward. As the camera panned over them Slocock was shocked to see that many of them showed signs of fungal infection. He glimpsed flashes of colored patches on their faces and hands but the cameraman, he noticed, didn't linger on any individual, either from personal distaste or official instruction. Probably the latter.

Then the blockade came into view—a row of military vehicles with men in full combat gear plugging the gaps. Whether they were police or troops it was impossible to tell. And all of them,

Slocock saw, were wearing gas masks and gloves. A lot of good that would do them, he reflected grimly.

There was a space of about 20 yards between the blockade and the column of evacuees. As those at the head of the column entered that space they were met by jets of water from water cannons mounted on trucks and tear gas bombs. Soldiers were also firing what appeared to be rubber bullets into the throng and Slocock thought he heard the distinctive crack of 7.62mm army rifles. The fact that there were several unmoving bodies in front of the blockade confirmed that real bullets were being used as well as rubber ones.

Faced with this impenetrable barrier, and being continually pushed forward by the surging mass behind them, the people at the front of the column were forced to scatter into the two side streets that ran parallel to the North Circular Road. Presumably they would try again to break through at other junctions where, no doubt, they would be met with the same resistance.

As Slocock watched the screen a car suddenly emerged from the end of the column and sped toward the barricade. The driver obviously had the futile idea of crashing his way through the line of army vehicles. But even before he'd got halfway, there was the rattle of a heavy machine gun. The car swerved sharply and plunged into the side of a house on the corner of the road. There was a muffled *whoof* and the car was obscured by a ball of fire.

Christ, thought Slocock. It came to this after only four days.

The camera abruptly panned upward to the sky. The commentator cried excitedly, "Something just happened above us to the north . . . yes, there it is!"

At the top of the screen an object could be seen turning over and over as it fell from the sky trailing black smoke. The camera closed in on it. It was a helicopter. It was burning fiercely and disintegrating as it fell. Pieces could clearly be seen breaking away from it. One of them looked disturbingly like a body . . .

"Yes, it's a helicopter!" cried the BBC reporter redundantly. "It appears to have been attacked by that jet fighter." The camera panned again, briefly catching a fast-moving dot in the distance. "An RAF Phantom, I think," said the reporter. "There have been rumors that various wealthy persons have been offering vast amounts of money to any helicopter pilot willing to come in, pick them up and fly them out of the quarantine area . . ." The camera returned to the falling helicopter and followed it all the way down until it disappeared behind some houses. A mushroom of smoke marked its point of impact.

"This puts a whole new light on the government's ban on commercial and private flights in and out of the restricted area," said the reporter. "Clearly they mean business."

The studio news reader reappeared on the screen. "We have just received information from sources in Northern Ireland that there are contingency plans to transfer the seat of British government to Stormont for the duration of the crisis. Sources at Westminster have neither confirmed nor denied the story.

"Nor can we get information on the physical condition of the Prime Minister and the members of her cabinet. Rumor has it that at least three cabinet ministers have fallen victim to the fungal plague but confirmation has not been forthcoming. However one reliable source claims that Mrs. Thatcher, several of her ministers, and senior government officials have, for the past two days, been residing in the nuclear bunkers below Whitehall.

"But our science correspondent, Tom Southern, believes that this measure doesn't offer much protection."

The camera cut to another man who a caption identified as Southern. He was a young, serious-looking character wearing thick glasses. "The problem is that fungi are the most prevalent and varied lifeform, apart from bacteria, known to man. One handful of soil probably contains about 10 to 20 million individual fungi either growing or in a dormant state. And a cubic meter of air can contain 180,000 spores.

"In other words we live in an environment saturated with fungi of different kinds, most of which we never notice in our daily lives . . . until now. The agent, whatever it is, that is causing all the trouble has the power to alter the genetic programming of *every* fungus spore it comes in contact with. It's acting like some cancer-causing virus within the fungi family, spreading from one species to another at an alarming rate.

"This means that all the government's attempts to block the spread of the infection are futile. It only takes one infected spore, or microscopic fungus particle, to transmit the virus to another species of fungi. And as I said, those species are all around us. Even in the sterile conditions of the Whitehall bunker there are no doubt tens of thousands of fungi spores. And it's likely that the virus has gained entrance to the bunker, carried in by one or more of the people taking shelter there. It could be in their lungs, their stomachs or their intestines.

"The grim truth is that unless we can rapidly isolate the cause of this plague and devise a means of counter acting it, we are *all* doomed, and that includes our leaders in their bunker."

He then held up his right hand which he'd previously kept behind his back. Slocock thought for a moment he was wearing a purple woolly mitten. Then he recognized what it was.

The screen abruptly went blank. There was silence for a time, then light background music began to play. A test card came up with the words THERE HAS BEEN A TEMPORARY FAULT. NORMAL TRANSMISSION WILL BE RESUMED AS SOON AS POSSIBLE.

Peterson got up and switched off the video machine. "That was the last news program from the BBC. The government accused them of spreading alarm and panic and pulled the plug. That was why this other program was recorded but never transmitted." He held up another video tape, then put it in the machine.

The screen came back to life. There was a title, CRISIS SPECIAL, then the camera cut to the harassed-looking face of a middle-aged man. "Good afternoon," he said quickly. "We have with us Dr. Bruce Carter from the Home Office. He was one of the first people to discover the outbreak and probably knows more about the nature of the plague than anyone else. But I must warn viewers that Dr. Carter has become a victim of a fungal infection himself."

The camera pulled back to show that the commentator was not alone. Sitting opposite him was . . .

Slocock felt the whiskey-engendered warmth in his body fade away. It was replaced with a deep chill that spread upwards along his spine and then through the rest of him. Worse, he suddenly felt sober.

Dr. Bruce Carter's head was covered with a series of overlapping brown, crusty slabs that had the texture of tree bark. The growths continued down his neck and disappeared into the collar of the loose-fitting shirt he was wearing. The shoulders of his jacket, which was also cut for someone several sizes larger than him, were grossly distorted by large bulges under the cloth.

Between the wart-like protuberances on his face his left eye could just be seen in one of the gaps. A crevice opened where his mouth should have been and Carter began to speak. He spoke with difficulty, his voice husky and wheezing. "I too would like to apologize for my appearance," he said slowly. "I wish I could say it's not as bad as it looks." He followed with a strange sound that must have been, astonishingly, laughter.

"Shit, he looks worse than the fucking Elephant Man," muttered Slocock.

"Shush!" ordered Peterson. "Pay attention, Sergeant."

"Dr. Carter," the interviewer on the screen was saying, "I understand you are of the firm belief that the plague is a man-made catastrophe and not a natural one."

Carter inclined his grotesque head. "Yes, I am," he wheezed. "If only one species of fungi had undergone a radical change in its metabolism and growth pattern then natural mutation might explain it, but the fact that *all* the species are being affected indicates an artificial agent." He paused to suck in air, then continued, "We must accept that what has happened is the result of a genetic engineering experiment that has gone hideously wrong."

"But who is responsible? Why don't they come forward and explain what they've done?"

"Maybe they were the first victims of their creation," said Carter. "Or they are in hiding, too afraid to admit what they've done. If the latter is so I plead with them to ring this number immediately." A telephone number was superimposed across the screen. "I have been empowered to offer them complete immunity from prosecution. It's imperative that we learn the exact chemical structure of the agent. Without that we can't begin to devise an effective means of counteracting it."

"Why hasn't it been possible to trace the whereabouts of the laboratory responsible?" asked the interviewer. "Surely there can't have been too many people doing research in this particular field."

"True," admitted Carter. "And in normal circumstances we would have pinpointed the source of the infection. But as you are well aware the circumstances are far from normal. Conditions here in London are already chaotic, and gaining access to records, and to people, is very difficult. But even so we are continuing to make progress in our investigations and I hope that we will have the answer very shortly."

"Do you give any credence to the rumor that this fungal plague might be deliberate?"

"You mean germ warfare?" Again the sound that was Carter's version of laughter. "A secret Russian attack and all that? I hardly think so. This is one weapon that will obviously rebound on its users. It doesn't recognize borders. It represents a threat to the entire world and I doubt if the Russians would have been so reckless to unleash it deliberately. Or even the Libyans who I've also heard mentioned."

"Just how fast is it spreading?"

"Very fast. But it would be spreading even faster if it wasn't for the fact that the virus or whatever has affected the reproductive cycles of the fungi. Normally a fungus will keep growing until it is time for it to send out its spores, but we've learned that the infected fungi species just continue growing without reaching the seeding stage. It's possible, however, that this stage may merely be postponed in the mutated species. They might start sporing tomorrow, next week, or next year. And when that happens it will be impossible to stop the plague from spreading rapidly around the world. A single fungal fruiting body, a mushroom's for example, can eject countless millions of spores into the air in just a few days."

The interviewer cleared his throat and said, "As a sufferer yourself what advice can you give to the viewers about the nature of the fungi that grow on people and the precautions one can take to prevent infection?"

"To be blunt there seems to be no effective way of preventing infection. Constant washing with antiseptics and disinfectants might provide you with brief protection against the various external fungi, but not against the ones that grow internally. The anti-fungal drugs, like nystatin, occasionally slow down the rate of infection but that's all. They don't provide a cure."

"But isn't it true that some people appear to be immune to infection?" The interviewer was clearly desperate to extract some note of optimism from Carter. But he was unsuccessful.

"It's too early to tell. It does seem that a small percentage might enjoy a natural immunity, but it's possible this is simply due to luck. We need more time to be sure."

"Isn't there any way of removing the fungus once it starts growing on you? Burning it off, for instance?"

"I'm afraid once you see any visible evidence of fungus infection it's too late. Burning away, or otherwise removing, the surface growth wouldn't affect the main part of the fungus. These growths you can observe on me, for example, are just the fruiting bodies. Most of the mycelium—the whole fungus—is below the surface, effectively rooted in me. Thousands of the thread-like roots are running through my body, feeding on me. The fungus is literally a *part* of me now. If I broke these fruiting bodies off I suspect I would die."

"Then you're saying that there's no hope for people who become infected?"

"There's no hope of killing the fungus without killing the host. But to become infected is not necessarily a death sentence. I consider myself one of the luckier victims. My fungus, though parasitic, appears to be of the benign variety—so far at least. Some fungi kill their hosts quickly, some drive them insane, but mine, inconvenient and as uncomfortable as it is, is letting me live. I'll just have to get used to it."

The interviewer did not seem reassured by Carter's calm fatalism. "You're saying mankind is completely helpless against the spread of the fungus?"

"Our only chance is to discover the exact chemical nature of the organic agent causing the plague. Once we know that, it's possible that scientists will be able to genetically engineer a neutralizing agent, in the form of a bacterium perhaps, that can be released into the environment.

"But unless we isolate the plague agent very soon, mankind is doomed."

The tape ended. The uneasy silence that followed was broken by Slocock saying loudly, "I say to hell with it. Let's forget the whole thing and get drunk instead."

7

"Don't be insubordinate, Sergeant!" Major Peterson said curtly. "This is a military operation and you're still in the army. You will maintain the correct attitude, or else!"

Slocock straightened in his chair. "Yessir. Sorry sir," he muttered.

Peterson glared at him then turned his attention to Wilson. "Dr. Wilson, permit me to introduce you to your traveling companions. Dr. Kimberley Fairchild and Sergeant Terence Slocock."

Wilson gave them both a distracted nod. Slocock guessed he hadn't recovered from the shock of the video tapes. That was understandable. Slocock didn't feel too steady himself.

Wilson lit another cigarette and said to Peterson, "It all seems hopeless. A suicide mission. All three of us will get infected with fungi before we have a chance to try and find Jane."

"Credit us with *some* foresight, Doctor," said Peterson. "Various steps have been taken to provide you with as much protection against the fungus as possible. A special vehicle is being prepared on the mainland which will contain all the necessary equipment to maintain a sterile, fungus-free environment. When you venture outside the vehicle you will wear an anti-contamination suit with its own air supply."

"Forgive me if I'm still not convinced. From what I've just seen and heard on those videos it's practically impossible to prevent infection."

Peterson cleared his throat and indicated Kimberley. "That's where Dr. Fairchild enters the picture. If you'd care to explain, Doctor?"

"There have been some developments in the time since Carter made that recording. One discovery that's been made is that a small percentage of people do seem to be immune to the fungi."

"How small is the percentage?" asked Wilson skeptically.

"Less than one percent," admitted Kimberley, "But even so that *is* encouraging."

"Yeah, sure. It means that out of every hundred people less than one person has a chance of survival." Wilson shook his head.

"What it *does* mean," said Kimberley, "is that the human immune system is capable of overcoming the fungi. In only rare cases, admittedly, but it's a hopeful sign. And it's possible that injections of inosine pranobex will provide us with extra protection."

Wilson frowned. "Inosine pranobex? I've never heard of it."

"It's new. It works by kicking the human immune system into action and produces an increase of T-lymphocyte cells. It's been found effective against certain forms of cancer."

"But does it work against the fungus?"

"It's being tested on the mainland. We don't have any results yet."

"Great," muttered Wilson. He stubbed his cigarette out and lit another one.

"But that's not all," continued Kimberley. "There's another drug we'll be using. Megacrine."

"I haven't heard of that one either."

"No way you could have. It's just been developed by some colleagues of mine at Bangor University. It's a chemically altered version of Mepacrine."

"That I *have* heard of."

"*I* haven't," cut in Slocock. He was beginning to feel excluded already. He had visions of having to listen to two egghead doctors discuss things he couldn't understand all the way to London.

"Mepacrine is an anti-malaria drug," said Kimberley. "It kills the parasitic organisms that infest the blood of malaria victims. It works by inserting its molecules into the DNA material of the malaria merozoites and preventing gene replication."

Slocock nodded, pretending he knew what the hell she was talking about.

"Megacrine has been genetically structured to do the same thing to the mutated fungus cells that enter the body," said Kimberley.

"Sounds like a major breakthrough," said Wilson. "But does it work?"

Kimberley's reply was guarded. "Well, it's worked on test animals at Bangor. And it's been partially successful on the few human guinea pigs who have tried it so far."

"Then why isn't this stuff being manufactured in bulk and being distributed to everyone on the mainland?" demanded Slocock.

"Two reasons. One is that it's not easy to synthesize. The second is that it's highly toxic. The doses have to be very carefully regulated. That's the main reason I'll be coming along on this expedition. To make sure you get the correct dosage. You'll need it injected intra-muscularly every 90 minutes."

Wilson regarded Kimberley suspiciously. "You said it was only partially successful on the human test subjects. What do you mean?"

Kimberley glanced at Major Peterson, then said reluctantly, "Of the four people it's been tested on so far two have died from the side effects."

"Shit," said Slocock.

"What exactly are the side effects?" asked Wilson.

But before Kimberley could answer, Major Peterson said hurriedly, "We can go into all that later. Let's continue with the briefing. Time is short. The boat taking you to the mainland leaves in just under an hour."

"Boat?" said Wilson, surprised. "Why aren't we going by plane?"

"Because the plane and aircrew would have to remain on the mainland. There's a strict quarantine around all of Britain. Any aircraft trying to leave is shot down by French or German fighters. I've no doubt I could get volunteers to take you over, but it would still be too risky. The airspace between here and the mainland is full of trigger-happy fly boys who often don't wait to see which direction a plane is flying before they shoot it down."

"I see," said Wilson slowly. Then, "What are the Yanks doing about all this?"

"For the moment, nothing. They're adopting a wait-and-see attitude. They aren't supporting the French in their call for more drastic quarantine measures. Probably because they've got a lot of their own people trapped on the mainland as well. The airlift of personnel from the American bases outside the infected areas had to be halted when the quarantine was imposed. But if the fungus keeps spreading the Americans will have no choice but to join in the French plan to drop nuclear bombs on Britain."

Wilson said nothing.

Peterson continued. "The boat will take you to Holyhead. From there you'll be flown to Bangor where you will undergo tests with the Megacrine drug until it's decided what doses you can tolerate individually. From there you'll be flown to Wolverhampton where your vehicle and other equipment will be waiting. Hopefully Wolverhampton will still be outside of the area of infection. From there you will proceed south to London."

"You make it sound easy," said Wilson. "But earlier you told me the people in the first search team were presumably attacked by mobs. What makes you think we won't suffer the same fate?"

"You'll be well armed," said O'Connell. It was the first time he'd spoken during the briefing. "Your vehicle will be fitted with both light and heavy machine guns."

Wilson turned to him. "Yes, but I'm obviously going to have to leave the vehicle on occasion once we get to London. What happens then?"

"Sergeant Slocock will be responsible for your protection," said O'Connell. Then he added with distaste, "He's quite an expert at that sort of thing."

Wilson gave Slocock a brief, curious glance.

"Once you reach the inner city," continued Peterson, "you will then carry out the search for your wife. You must discover where she went after she removed all the records from her lab."

"But you don't know for certain that it was her. It could have been one of her assistants."

The major nodded. "Carter mentioned them in his final radio message. Said there were three of them. Got their names but not their addresses. By that time it was impossible to obtain even basic information—the system had collapsed completely. Do you know these people and where they lived?"

"I've met all three, but I only know the address of one of them."

"Which one?"

Wilson paused before answering. "Hilary Burne-Smith. She has, or *had*, a flat in Islington. In Upper Street."

Slocock, observing the vaguely uncomfortable expression on Wilson's face, smiled to himself. Sounded as if the doc had been getting his rocks off with the triple-barreled name case.

"Then check that out too," said Peterson, standing up and gathering his papers together. "Sorry to rush you but it's time you were leaving for the harbor. Captain O'Connell will escort you there. I wish you good luck on your mission."

"Hang on," said Wilson. "There's one important thing you haven't mentioned. Say we succeed; we find my wife or her notes and radio the information to you, but then what happens? How do we get back?"

Slocock laughed. "Haven't you caught on yet, Wilson? There's no return ticket. It's a one-way trip."

8

The Hastings Branch of the International Socialist League was called to order. It consisted of three people. Comrade Henderson was in the chair. Comrade Snell was taking minutes. And Comrade Blakey made up the rest of the branch. Under other circumstances the branch would have been bigger. But considering the particular and peculiar situation, three was a pretty good turn-out.

"Comrades," said Geoffrey Henderson, his shadow jumping about on the sandstone wall as the candle flickered. "We have a crisis."

All three of them were well aware of the crisis but as usual Geoffrey was intent on going through the formalities. Sheena Blakey listened with only a fraction of her attention, partly because she knew what he was going to say and partly because she was wondering which one of her two Comrades was going to want to demonstrate his solidarity to her that night.

The previous night she'd been obliged to accommodate both of them. After arguing over whose turn it was with her they'd had a vote to suspend the normal rota system temporarily. Sheena had lost by two votes to one. She had a strong suspicion there'd be a similar vote tonight.

She was beginning to wish she'd never come down with them into the caves, but it had seemed a good idea at the time. At first, when the news of the fungus had reached Hastings, most people had seen it as a problem for London alone. Despite the warnings on TV and radio, and the local government's attempts to take preparatory action, it seemed like one of those things that would simply go away or never affect Hastings. But then things changed.

She wasn't quite sure when, but suddenly people began panicking. All but the most elderly or stubborn inhabitants tried to get out of town, with or without their belongings. But there was nowhere to go. It was the same everywhere. The people in the other towns and villages—nearby St. Leonards, Bexhill, Bulverhythe, and Crowhurst—were panicking too. There were fights, riots, and general chaos throughout the area.

Oh, some people tried to leave in fishing boats and anything else they could get their hands on, either paying the high prices the fishermen set or resorting to violence to hijack the craft. But it wasn't long before the French navy put a stop to that. Word soon got back that the Frogs were sinking every boat that went beyond the three-mile limit. And without even giving any of them a chance to turn back.

It was then that Geoff came up with his plan. It was blindingly simple. They would go and live in the caves.

Under the West Cliff were four caves, partly carved from the sandstone by prehistoric streams but mostly by man for commercial reasons; sand for glass and holes for tourists.

No sand had been removed for glass-making for over a hundred years, and there were certainly no tourists around at the moment, so Geoff's scheme was for the Hastings Branch of the ISL to retreat into the caves with plenty of supplies and wait there until the fungus problem was over. He thought of it as a scourge sent to scour Britain clean of Toryism. After it had done that it would, like the Biblical flood, disappear and the ISL would surface to take charge of the new world.

In the event only two members of the ISL had been smart

enough to follow Geoff into the caves. The other four had decided to take their chances above ground. *Smart?* Sheena was having her doubts if that was the right word. Perhaps the other four were the smart ones.

Before retreating underground they had, on Geoff's orders, broken into a supermarket and taken lots of canned food, candles, and dozens of bottles of spring water. They'd also broken into a camping store and stolen sleeping bags, a kerosene stove, and some gas lamps.

At the caves they made some effort to barricade the entrance, then settled down to life below the surface. For the first few days Sheena found it fun. A bit of an adventure. But then boredom quickly set in. They couldn't get a peep out of the radio they'd brought with them, and the books that Geoff had insisted on selecting on their behalf were either by or about Karl Marx.

Not that much reading would have been possible even if she had had a more appetising range of books; the electric lights had gone out by the end of the first week and then they'd used up all the gas for the lamps. Now they were reduced to the dim light of the candles, and their supply of those was fast dwindling too.

Geoff and Horace kept themselves occupied by discussing Marxist theory and taking turns in her sleeping bag. At first so much sex had been a mild novelty for her but the novelty had soon palled and now she was fed up with being continually screwed by two incompetents. Her big hope was that they'd get bored with heterosexual sex and start screwing each other.

However she couldn't deny that Geoff's idea had worked. They made regular checks of the caves but there was no evidence of any fungus. Geoff had reasoned that the fungus wouldn't "bother"—he almost endowed it with sentience when he spoke about it—to go underground. Nothing to eat and too cold for it, he insisted. It probably didn't like sandstone, Sheena decided. She didn't like it much herself.

But now the crisis had arisen. They were running short of water as well as candles. They had planned to drink the water from the cave's public toilets, but an investigation had shown that the water now entering the cisterns was a very strange color. The bottled water they had left would last three people only a couple of more days. They had no option but to make a journey to the surface.

The meeting had been called to decide who should go. Sheena knew it wouldn't be Geoff. Most likely it would be her, but if Geoff decided he didn't want to risk losing the only woman in the group then Horace would be the unlucky one. Poor Horace. Horace Snell. What a name for a 25-year-old Marxist revolutionary. But it suited him. He *was* a Horace.

Sheena's main worry was that Geoff might miss arguing Marxist theory with Horace more than he'd miss sex with her. After all, the former occupied him for hours at a time while the latter took him two minutes, at best. Prerevolutionary ejaculation, she called it—although not to his face.

It was time to vote.

The result was as she feared. She lost two to one.

They both stared at her expectantly. "Well, off you go, Sheena," said Geoff. "If you go now you can be back by nightfall."

She came to a decision. "Up yours, Geoff," she said calmly. "I'm not going anywhere."

They both looked profoundly shocked. "But we've had a vote," protested Horace. "You *have* to go."

"I'm not going and you can't make me so that's that."

They tried to argue with her for several minutes but all she did was shake her head and repeat that she wasn't going anywhere.

Finally Geoff said to her sorrowfully, "I'm very, *very* disappointed in you, Sheena. You're not just letting us down, you're letting down the whole of the International Socialist League."

"Screw the International Socialist League. I've decided to become an anarchist."

Geoff stiffened. He said sternly, "Sheena, you leave me no choice but to expel you from the Hastings Branch of the League. Take your things and leave immediately."

"Expel until you're blue in the face, Geoff. I'm not leaving the cave."

He sighed and turned to Snell. "I'm afraid you'll have to go instead, Horace."

"*Me?*" It was almost a yelp.

"Well, I certainly can't go. As League coordinator for the

entire Hastings area I'm far too important to the Cause to be put at risk."

Snell obviously wanted to discuss this further. Indeed he looked as if he would like to have discussed it at great length, but instead he reluctantly got to his feet, picked up one of the remaining candle stubs, and made his way slowly out of the cave. "I'll be back as soon as I can," he told them, hopefully.

He was some way from the entrance to the caves when the candle went out. He couldn't see a thing but he was confident he knew where he was. Just before the light had gone he'd seen the big fissure where the tiny ends of beech tree roots had found their way some sixty feet underground.

He walked on, hand brushing lightly against the slightly crumbly cave wall. Suddenly something touched his face—something wet and cold. Slimy. He reached up to brush it away.

The next thing he knew his wrist had been seized in some kind of loop that tightened painfully and, at the same time, started to pull his hand up toward the ceiling.

With a panicky yell he grabbed at the thing with his other hand with the aim of wrenching himself free. He found himself holding something the thickness of a strand of macaroni. A snake, he wondered as he pulled on it as hard as he could. But whatever it was didn't give way. Instead he continued to be hauled inexorably upward.

He screamed as he felt another loop tighten around the bicep of his other arm. A third loop snaked around his right forearm.

Screaming and kicking, he was pulled upward until he could no longer touch the ground with his feet.

He screamed even louder as something sharp began to bore itself into the side of his stomach. After that came an explosion of intolerable agony.

A short time later he was dead.

In the bottom cave Geoff and Sheena heard his screams. When they'd started Geoff had looked fearfully at Sheena and said, "Jesus, Sheen, you'd better go see what's happening . . ."

"Me. No way. You go. You're the man."

"That's a pretty reactionary, not to mention sexist, thing to say!"

She simply shrugged.

The screams changed pitch. It no longer sounded like Horace, but some animal being burnt alive.

"Look, how about we *both* go?" cried Geoff, his eyes bulging with alarm.

She thought it over and nodded. "But only if you take the lead," she said firmly.

The screaming had ceased by the time they started to move. They progressed warily through the series of caves, Geoff stopping several times when his flickering candle produced menacing, shadowy shapes ahead of them. He was holding the nearest thing to a weapon they had—a small axe. Sheena stayed well behind him despite his requests for her to close the gap between them.

Finally they reached Horace.

He dangled from the ceiling of the cave where it was split by the fissure. He was held in a network of glistening white strands that reminded Sheena of thick spaghetti or macaroni. Several of them had formed tight loops around his body. Others appeared to be growing *into* it.

He was almost unrecognizable. He was grotesquely bloated as if he'd been pumped up with air. His thin face had gone perfectly round and his fingers were like bunches of white carrots.

"Jesus, what *are* those things?" gasped Geoff, moving closer. "What happened to him?"

Sheena looked up and saw that the "spaghetti" extended down from the ends of the beech tree roots. "Don't go near him," she warned Geoff.

"Shit, we can't leave him hanging there like that. I'm going to cut him down." He walked up to Horace's suspended body and raised the axe.

"Geoff!" she yelled.

But it was too late. The white strands, which had been perfectly motionless, suddenly sprang into life as Geoff neared them. Before he could react a white loop had appeared round his hand holding the axe. He tried to jerk free but other loops snared his left arm.

"Sheena, help me!"

But she could only stand there and watch as the white strands wrapped themselves around him in increasing numbers, their loops constricting his limbs.

She didn't know it but she was watching a mutated form of *arthrobotrys oligospora* in action. One of the carnivorous fungi, it had been previously restricted to microscopic size in the soil where it fed on small worms called nematodes. It trapped the worms within the ringed snares strung along its adhesive network of hyphae and then used a penetration knob to enter their bodies, pump toxin into them, and spread out a cluster of special feeding hyphae that grew out along the length of the worms' bodies. These hyphae would liquefy the worms' tissues and absorb the digested food until only the skins remained.

This is what had happened to Horace Snell, and was in the process of happening to Geoffrey Henderson . . .

The mutated *arthrobotrys oligospora* penetrated his writhing body in several places with the sharp pegs on the ends of its hyphae and then began to inject a toxin to incapacitate him. As the toxin was pure ammonia Geoff's discomfort was acute.

Sheena waited until Geoff was silent and his body had begun to swell. Then she turned and headed back toward the end cave.

Once there she stretched out on her sleeping bag and put her hands behind her head. "Peace at last," she murmured.

9

The Belfast dock area was crawling with soldiers.

As they halted at yet another roadblock Wilson was struck by the futility of all this military activity. What did the Army hope to achieve by the show of force? What use were guns against microscopic particles of fungi being wafted ashore in the wind? Or perhaps a seabird landing on some remote stretch of coast would bring the fungus to Ireland. He guessed this display of military muscle was more for the benefit of the officers and soldiers themselves than anyone else. By strutting around and being obtuse in the way typical of all British authority they were fooling themselves into thinking they still had some control over the situation.

The discussion between the officer in charge of the roadblock and O'Connell went on and on. Finally the officer disappeared into a small hut by the side of the road. The pole remained lowered in front of their vehicle.

"What's all this for?" Wilson asked O'Connell. "Couldn't you have phoned ahead or something? It would be nice to go to our deaths without being held up by army red tape."

"It's regulations," said O'Connell curtly. "They're only doing their job."

"Their job?" Wilson laughed. "I suppose they'll still be checking each other's passes when they're nothing but toadstools on legs."

"That's not funny," said O'Connell.

"It wasn't meant to be."

It was the last of the roadblocks. Once through, the army staff car turned onto a wharf and pulled up alongside a strange-looking boat. It was about 90 feet long and had a square, chunky shape to it apart from the bow and forward cabin which were streamlined. It also seemed to sit very low in the water.

"Christ, what kind of tub is that?" exclaimed Slocock as they got out of the car. "It'll take us forever to get to England in that thing."

"On the contrary," said a man in naval uniform who was coming along the gangway leading from the top deck of the vessel. "This is *HMS Speedy*, the Royal Navy's first hydrofoil in nearly 40 years. As we can't fly you to the mainland this is the next best thing." He held out his hand. "I'm Captain Barclay. Welcome aboard."

They all shook hands with him except for Slocock who said, "No offense, Captain, but it's a habit I've picked up recently. Avoid all physical contact with someone until you know where they've been."

Captain Barclay regarded him with amusement. "Probably a wise precaution where you're going. Rather you than me, I must admit. I admire your courage. All of you."

"Courage has nothing to do with it," muttered Wilson. Then he added, "But won't you be stuck on the mainland too, after you've delivered us?"

"No. I'm dropping you a half a mile outside of Holyhead. You'll go the rest of the way in that." He pointed to one of two rubber boats lashed to the roof of the cabin. Both of them had powerful-looking outboard motors.

"Time you were leaving," said O'Connell, glancing at his watch.

"Not coming with us?" asked Slocock, an edge to his voice. "I thought you'd want to make sure we reach our destination."

"Captain Barclay is more than capable of doing that," he said stiffly. "Goodbye, and good luck. I don't have to tell you how much depends on the success of your mission."

"No, you don't," said Wilson. He muttered farewell to O'Connell and followed the others up the gangway and onto the deck of the hydrofoil. The gangway was immediately pushed ashore by crewmen who then began to cast off.

Barclay led them into the spacious bridge. Two other naval officers were there. One of them sat facing controls that were more like those of an aircraft than a boat. Barclay nodded to him.

"Okay Jim, take her away," he said casually. He obviously ran an informal ship.

An engine rumbled into life and the vessel started to move. Wilson looked back at O'Connell's stiff, unmoving figure on the wharf. He's a dead man already, thought Wilson, and we soon will be.

The hydrofoil moved slowly out of the harbor and into Belfast Lough. Then it began to pick up speed.

"I'm afraid it's going to be a noisy and bumpy ride once we're up on our foils," warned Captain Barclay. "I think you'll be more comfortable down below. We can't offer much in the way of passenger amenities but I can at least give you a drink or three."

Slocock's face brightened. "Thank God for the Navy," he said.

Barclay waited until *HMS Speedy* had lifted herself out of the water and was riding on her three foils, propelled by her two gas-turbine water jets at a speed of over 45 knots, before he led them below.

"She's a great little boat," he said proudly as he ushered them into a small cabin fitted with comfortable chairs, a couch and a card table. "She was supposed to be the first of a fleet of five but the budget cuts put an end to that."

He told them to sit down and then produced a bottle of Johnny Walker and four glasses.

As Wilson sipped his scotch and listened to Barclay make small-talk about Defense Budgets he experienced a sudden feeling of unreality. Not many hours ago he'd been working as usual in his County Wicklow cottage and now he was plunged into a nightmare world where London had been practically destroyed and all human life was under threat. And he, Barry Wilson, failed scientist and struggling writer, was expected somehow to save the day. All he had to do was make a long journey into an unimaginably poisonous environment with two complete strangers and find his wife, who, if she was still alive, could be anywhere in what remained of London.

I'll wake up, he told himself. *I'll wake up and be back in my own safe world where my biggest problem is thinking up ways to stall my bank manager.*

But he didn't wake up. He remained stuck in the small cabin in the hydrofoil that was juddering like a bus being driven at speed over very rough ground.

For the first time he looked closely at his two traveling companions. Slocock didn't impress him. He looked like a thug. A tough thug. Someone who'd be dangerous in a fight, despite his small stature. Wilson didn't relish the thought of being trapped in close proximity with him for any length of time.

On the other hand Kimberley Fairchild looked very attractive. He hadn't realized until then just how attractive she was. Beautiful skin, good, strong features and an interesting body. He wondered what it would look like out of those baggy clothes.

He glanced up to find she was looking straight at him. "I met your wife once, Dr. Wilson," she said.

"Really? When?" he asked. He was sure she knew what he'd been thinking.

"Two years ago. At a mycology conference in London. At London University. She impressed me a great deal. I could easily believe what people said about her—that she was a genius in her field."

"Some genius," said Slocock with a bitter laugh.

Wilson didn't know what to say. He felt an instinctive urge to defend Jane, but how could he? The enormity of what she'd done hung over them like a giant cloud. A *mushroom* cloud, he thought bleakly. What was worse was that he felt a certain guilt-by-association. He knew it was irrational but he couldn't help it.

"It must have been terrible for her," said Kimberley.

Wilson frowned. "How do you mean?"

"When she realized what she'd done. After years of effort trying to create something that would benefit all mankind she discovers her work has produced the very opposite effect. The knowledge must have devastated her."

"Look, I know she's your wife and all, mate," said Slocock, "But as far as I'm concerned," he turned to Kimberley, "I'm not wasting any sympathy on her. She's a typical bloody scientist, pissing about with things she didn't understand and dropping us all in the shit as a result."

"Uh, anyone like another drink?" Captain Barclay broke in diplomatically. Slocock of course said yes.

Wilson asked Barclay when they'd reach Holyhead.

"Should take us about two and a half hours, barring delays along the way."

"What sort of delays?"

"Well, I expect we'll run into our prickly French friends. The top brass has informed them of our mission and theoretically we've got clearance both ways. But you know what the French are like. I may be doing them a disservice but I have the strong feeling that the French have been waiting for a chance like this ever since the Battle of Trafalgar."

They had their first encounter with the French an hour into their journey. An intercom that Wilson hadn't noticed gave a shrill squawk and a voice said urgently, "Captain, you're needed on the bridge."

Barclay hurried out. After a hesitant pause Wilson decided to follow him. Slocock and Kimberley got up too.

The hydrofoil was already slowing down when they reached the bridge. As Wilson looked out he was alarmed to see a large geyser of water explode out of the sea about 50 yards directly ahead of them. He realized it was a shell.

Then he saw the other vessel. It lay a quarter of a mile on their port side. A destroyer, he decided, or a corvette.

One of the officers handed Barclay a pair of binoculars. "It's the *Montcalm*, sir. That's the second time they've lobbed a 100mm at us. I've raised them on the blower but all they're speaking is French."

Barclay took a quick look through the glasses then snatched up the headset sitting on top of the radio. He spoke rapidly in French. Wilson saw a puff of smoke appear at the front of the French ship. Shortly afterwards another plume of water shot out of the sea ahead of the hydrofoil, but this time much closer. There was a dull boom.

The hydrofoil was now settling into the water and coming to a stop.

The next shell, Wilson realized, would blow them apart.

Barclay's torrent of French grew louder in volume. Then he dropped the headset back on the radio and heaved a sigh of relief. "A close one," he said. "But I think I've convinced them of our identity. Very reluctant to believe me, though."

"Couldn't they tell we were heading toward England instead of away from it?" Wilson asked.

"No. We're traveling due south at the moment so we could have come from anywhere. Like Scotland perhaps. The French are obviously not taking chances anymore."

HMS Speedy started moving again and was soon back on its foils. Wilson watched the French ship anxiously but there were no more puffs of smoke.

They didn't encounter another French vessel until they were approaching the three-mile limit, though they had been buzzed on several occasions by both jet fighters and helicopters. This one was a much smaller craft but moved almost as fast as the hydrofoil.

"It's a Combattante," explained Barclay. "One of their new fast strike craft. Can do 35 knots and it's armed with four MM.38 Exocets. It's going to follow us in and make sure we don't go any closer to the mainland than we said we would."

As the hydrofoil continued on toward the coast Barclay pointed out wreckage floating in the water. "They've been busy around here recently."

They passed more wreckage. And bodies. Burnt bodies floating face-down.

Then they passed someone who was still alive. It was a man, his face black from either burns or oil. He waved feebly. Barclay glanced at him and then stared grimly ahead.

"You're just going to leave him there?" asked Wilson.

"I have to. I stop and pick him up those Frenchmen behind us will blow us out of the water."

Wilson looked back at the man who was still waving, then he turned and stared ahead too. He tried to rationalize his guilt by telling himself there was worse to come.

It was just after 6 p.m. when they halted at the half-mile point. The July sun was still hot on Wilson's face as he went out on deck. The rubber boat was being made ready by four of the *Speedy's* crew. In the distance he could see that the French patrol boat had also come to a halt. It looked ominous.

"Sea's like a millpond so you shouldn't have any trouble getting ashore," said Barclay with forced brightness. "Anyway I understand they'll be sending a launch out to meet you. We'll radio that you're on your way."

When the rubber boat was in the water the three of them said goodbye to Barclay and climbed down into it. Slocock started the outboard motor.

Wilson watched the hydrofoil recede into the distance with a tremendous feeling of regret. Despite the French gunboats and aircraft he had felt secure in the company of Barclay and his men. Now he was on his own. Well, almost.

He glanced at Kimberley. "What have you got in store for us tonight, Doctor? When we reach Bangor, I mean."

"I told you. We start you on a course of the Megacrine drug," she said guardedly.

"Yes, but will we have time for a few hours' relaxation? A restaurant meal, perhaps? Or a visit to a pub? My treat."

"I don't think you'll feel like either eating *or* boozing."

"Why? Are the side effects of the drug that bad?"

"They're not good."

"So tell me, what are they?"

"Do you really want to know?"

"I'll have to know sooner or later."

"Yeah, tell us, Doc," called Slocock from the stern of the boat. "Do we turn purple or what?"

Kimberley sighed. "Megacrine produces the following side-effects: nausea, vomiting, abdominal cramps, headache, diarrhea, vertigo, excessive sweating, fever, itching, insomnia, and pains in all the muscles and joints. And if the dosage is too strong for your individual metabolism it can seriously damage your skin, your gastro-intestinal tract and central nervous system with potentially fatal results. Satisfied?"

"Christ," muttered Wilson.

"I think I'd prefer to turn into a mushroom," said Slocock.

10

Wilson screwed his eyes shut and tensed his muscles as the now familiar spasms started again. But he couldn't prevent the stream of vomit bursting from his mouth. Most of it missed the bucket and spattered on the floor. He couldn't have cared less. He felt close to death.

He was lying on a bed in a hall of residence at Bangor University. It was nearly 4 a.m. and Kimberley's medical colleagues had been injecting the damned anti-fungus drug into him for over six hours now. He had no idea whether he was having a good or bad reaction to the stuff, nor did he know how either Kimberley or Slocock were faring. All he knew was that he'd never felt so bad in all his life.

They'd arrived in Holyhead just before 7 p.m. and Wilson had been immediately struck by how different it was from Belfast. Like Belfast the place was crawling with soldiers, but whereas the atmosphere in Belfast had been tense and anxious, here it was much worse. There was an air of despair in Holyhead and, more disturbing, an underlying sense of panic. The soldiers were all acting very nervously, glancing about continually with suspicious eyes. They clutched their guns as if they were magic talismans that could somehow protect them against the fungus. Wilson felt that it wouldn't take much of a spark to set them off. They'd run amok, shooting at everything.

As Wilson and the others, with their armed escort, moved through the series of cordons, they were regarded with undisguised hostility when the soldiers discovered who they were. It puzzled Wilson at first—he wondered if it was because he was Jane Wilson's husband—but then he presumed it was because the three of them had come from Ireland which the trapped masses in Holyhead and elsewhere along the coast looked upon as a tantalizingly close but unreachable haven of safety. They resented anyone who could be so crazy as to leave the place and actually come to the mainland.

Even the members of their escort—an MI5 official and two Special Branch men—were cold and unfriendly toward them. Wilson tried pumping them for information about the present situation inland but only received unhelpful monosyllabic answers.

Just by looking around as their vehicle pushed its way through the choked streets Wilson could tell how bad the situation had become. Refugees outnumbered the soldiers ten-to-one. They milled around helplessly, trapped between the approaching fungus and the military lines guarding the seafront.

"Don't see why you don't just turn the poor bastards loose and let them take their chances with the French," said Slocock as they passed by a crowd of refugees trying to push their way through a barricade.

"Because the more people who try and escape by sea, the more likely the Frogs will start dropping neutron bombs on us," said one of the Special Branch men.

There were groups of refugees all along the road to Bangor and Bangor itself was also packed with people.

At Bangor University they were met by Kimberley's colleague, Dr. George Helman, a fat, feminine-looking man with a wispy blond mustache and delicate hands. He and Kimberley greeted each other like long-lost friends and Wilson experienced a slight twinge of jealousy as he watched them hug each other. Former lovers, he wondered? It was difficult to imagine Kimberley making love to this bizarre character but perhaps she was the sort of woman who found intelligent men a turn-on. If that was the case then Wilson decided he stood a better chance of getting somewhere with her than Slocock. He'd already noticed a certain antagonism between them.

After showing them their quarters and giving them a half hour to "freshen up," as Helman put it, he took them into a laboratory where tests were being run on samples of the mutated fungi. Through two layers of thick glass they watched people encased in bulky white suits at work in the sealed-off area.

"Bit risky, isn't it?" Wilson asked him. "All you need is for one mutated cell to get out and you'll have brought the plague here as well."

"Those people you see in there are all volunteers. They never come out. They have a separate living area sealed off from the lab but the whole complex is cut off from the outside world. *Nothing* comes out of there. Air is recycled, waste products are stored . . . not a single molecule of anything gets out of there."

"Still risky, though. What if there's an accident? A faulty seal? Or someone just makes a stupid human error?"

"We have to take that risk, Dr. Wilson," said Helman. "The only labs where research is being carried out on actual samples of the fungus are all located in this country. No one yet wants to take the chance of importing samples into other countries, for the very reasons you've just listed."

"You still haven't isolated the cause of the plague?"

"No. But thanks to you we're now following up a new line of attack."

Wilson frowned. "Me?"

"Your information about the enzymes. It was passed on to us from Belfast. And to every other lab working on the problem. I've no doubt one of us will crack it sooner or later, but 'later' is something we just can't afford. That's why it's vital you get your hands on the precise chemical breakdown of the agent."

"You don't have to remind me," said Wilson brusquely. If one more person told him the fate of mankind rested on his shoulders he'd go berserk.

"Has any progress been made in finding ways of killing the stuff?" he asked.

"Oh, killing the fungi is easy," said Helman. "It's stopping it from spreading that's the problem. The army and air force have been dumping all kinds of things on the infected areas—everything from napalm to Agent Orange—and have had a lot of success, but only temporarily.

"When it was clear that London was a write-off they created a mile-wide barrier right around the city. Everything in that zone was razed, burned and sprayed with poison. Planes and helicopters continually sprayed more poison over the area but still the fungi got out."

"How far has it spread now?" asked Slocock.

"It's covering most of southern England. It's reached the coast from Southend all the way round to Torquay . . . Cornwall and parts of Devon are still uninfected but probably not for much longer. Northward it's as far as Warwick. It's moving on a curved front that stretches from southern Wales through Hereford and Worcester, Warwick, Northampton, Cambridgeshire and Suffolk.

"But there are other, smaller, areas of infection further north. In Derby, Yorkshire . . . there's even one in Scotland."

They were all silent for a time. Then Kimberley said, "What success have you had in treating victims of the fungus?"

"Practically none," admitted Helman. "Come, I'll show you."

He led them into a different room. There the observation panel looked in on a section of the laboratory that contained a number of cages. Things were moving in the cages but Wilson couldn't tell what they were. They appeared to be shapeless, fuzzy blobs. One of them was simply a cluster of spherical white toadstools that staggered blindly about the cage.

"What are they?" he asked.

"Cats."

"I wish you hadn't told me that."

"Each one is infected with a different species of fungi. We've tried everything but we can't kill the fungus without killing the host."

"What about radiation?" asked Kimberley.

"Yes." Helman nodded his chubby face. "We have had some good results with that, but the level of radiation needed to kill all of the deep-rooted hyphal strands is inevitably fatal for the host. And even if you could find a safe way of killing the fungi, the infestation leaves the host in a pretty ravaged state. Large sections of skin eaten away, serious damage to the internal organs from the penetrating hyphae, and so on.

"It's only really in the area of prevention that we've had any real success. Megacrine is our star performer."

He took them into another section. Through the thick glass they saw a middle-aged man wearing jeans and t-shirt, lying on a bed reading. "He's been exposed to fungi infection for several days but so far there's been no sign of it in his body," said Helman.

"He doesn't look too hot," observed Slocock sourly.

"Apart from the side effects of the drug he's also dying of a tumor in the brain. That's why he volunteered for this."

"I understand you lost two of your four volunteers who took the drug," said Wilson.

"Uhhh, yes, but that was before we realized that individual tolerances to it varied greatly. I'm confident we can treat each of you without endangering your lives. However, the side-effects . . ." he paused and looked inquiringly at Kimberley.

"I've told them it won't be pleasant," said Kimberley.

"Well, I suppose we'd better get on with it then," said Helman apologetically.

"How about a bite to eat first?" asked Slocock. "I'm bloody starving."

Helman looked uncomfortable. "I don't think food would be a good idea," he said.

That had been the understatement of the decade, thought Wilson as he got off the bed and staggered toward the toilet. His guts were on fire again and he could hardly stand. He got his pants down and collapsed onto the seat just in time. The little control he had over his bowels went and with a searing pain his rectum released what felt like sulphuric acid.

Afterwards he sat there trembling, too weak to move. His head throbbed appallingly and his limbs ached. *I'm dying*, he told himself. *I hope*.

When he'd finally managed to get himself back to the bed the door opened and Helman entered to make one of his periodic checks on Wilson's condition.

"How are we feeling now?" he asked cheerfully as he put the cold end of a stethoscope onto Wilson's sweaty chest.

"*We* are feeling fucking terrible. We are feeling even more fucking terrible than the last time you asked me."

Helman made a clucking sound. "Now, now, Dr. Wilson, you should think yourself fortunate. Your reaction to Megacrine has been relatively mild."

"Mild? Why, you great, fat, crazy . . ."

"Yes, *mild*. We almost lost poor Kim."

"Kim?" Wilson's mind had gone blank. "Who the hell's Kim?"

"Kimberley. Her heart stopped. Luckily we got it going again within less than a minute. No serious damage, thank God. She should recover all right."

"Her *heart* stopped?" gasped Wilson as the meaning of the words sunk in.

Helman nodded. "It was a close thing."

"Jesus," whispered Wilson.

"The Sergeant seems to be pulling through okay though. His reaction has been even less severe than yours."

"That's marvelous," muttered Wilson. He didn't give a damn about Slocock. But Kimberley . . . the extent of the shock he felt on hearing she'd almost died surprised him. With her along the journey ahead had seemed almost bearable, but to have to make it alone with Slocock was unthinkable. Especially feeling like this.

He shook his head wearily. "How the hell are we going to travel any distance in this condition? I feel so weak I can hardly stand and from what you say Kimberley must be a lot worse."

"This is just the initial reaction. You'll feel better as your body adjusts. You won't feel *well*, of course, and if there's a mistake in your dosage these acute symptoms could recur, but I should say you'll be fit enough to travel by tomorrow night."

He took out a syringe and asked Wilson to roll up his sleeve. "I'm going to take another blood sample. If the test results are good I'll give you something that will knock you out for a while. By the time you wake up you should feel much better."

Wilson woke up feeling terrible. True, he didn't feel as sick as before, but he still felt pretty bad. It was like a combination of the worst hangover of his life with an influenza attack. The thought of walking a few yards, much less flying to Wolverhampton, definitely did not appeal to him.

He pressed the buzzer beside the bed. Shortly Helman came

bouncing into the room, looking as cherubic as ever. Wilson remembered the fungus-covered cats in the laboratory.

"Ah, good! You look *lots* better." He gave Wilson a quick examination and then said, "Come and see the others. They're awake too."

Feeling dizzy, Wilson followed Helman unsteadily down the corridor and into Kimberley's room. She was propped up in bed and talking to Slocock, who was sitting on the end of the bed.

Wilson's irritation at seeing them on obviously better terms was overshadowed by the shock of Kimberley's appearance. He could barely recognize her. She looked shattered. Her face was pasty and haggard and her eyes were sunken and surrounded by black rings.

She gave him a weak smile. "Hello Barry, how are you feeling?" Her voice was like an old woman's.

Ignoring her, Wilson turned angrily on Helman. "This is ridiculous!" he cried. "She *can't* travel in that condition!"

Helman spread his hands helplessly. "I'm afraid she has to."

"No, I won't permit it! The Sergeant and I will have to go by ourselves!"

"You'd never reach London without me," said Kimberley. "Without me to regulate the dosages of Megacrine you'd quickly become incapacitated."

"I don't care," said Wilson. "It's out of the question. I refuse to let you come with us."

Helman pursed his cupid's bow lips. "I'm afraid, Dr. Wilson, that you have no choice in the matter."

Five hours later, after they'd rested and managed to keep down some soup, they climbed into the army Lynx helicopter that was to take them to Wolverhampton. This time they were accompanied by only the dour MI5 official.

Kimberley had improved a little but still looked terribly ill. She sat in the helicopter with her eyes tightly closed as if using all her willpower not to throw up.

Helman stood there waving as the helicopter lifted off.

Wilson didn't wave back.

11

"What is it?" asked Wilson.

"It *was* a 'Stalwart'," said Slocock. "An Alvis PV2 'Stalwart' Mark 3." He was impressed. Someone had done a hell of a lot of work on it in a very short time.

They were standing in a shed at a make-shift army camp on the outskirts of Wolverhampton. The center of attention was a large, six-wheeled army truck. It stood very high off the ground on its huge balloon tires, its angular front similar to that of a landing craft. It was amphibious and its built-in propulsion units could, Slocock knew, push it through still water at four to five knots. Slocock had driven one before—there were not many vehicles in the British army he hadn't driven—but he'd never seen a Stalwart quite like this one.

Its rear freight section had been completely encased in what appeared to be half-inch armor and supported a gun mount. There was a smaller gun mount on the roof of the driver's cabin. But the internal modifications were even more surprising, as Slocock saw when their temporary host at the camp, Major Buxton, showed them inside the back compartment.

To get in you had to go through a small airlock, just big enough for one person at a time. "When this is operating your anti-contamination suit will be sprayed with a powerful disinfectant as you come through," he explained. "Make sure you wash all the stuff off before you proceed into the living section. I'm told it's highly toxic.

"Sorry it's a bit cramped in here but we had to cram a lot of extra gear into a limited space. Those bulges running under the two bunks are the spare fuel tanks. Fifty gallons in each."

"Only two bunks," said Wilson, "but there are three of us."

"The third person will have to sleep in the driver's cabin. But I doubt if it would be wise for all three of you to sleep at the same time."

Slocock automatically swung his kit onto one of the bunks.

There was a clink of bottles as the bag landed. Buxton raised an eyebrow but said nothing. Slocock had been breathing whiskey fumes on everyone since his arrival. During the chopper ride he'd got through a third of a bottle. It didn't do much for his stomach or his throbbing head but at least it dulled the nagging pains in his arms and legs.

Most of the space was taken up by oxygen cylinders. "Your air here and in the driver's cabin will be recycled, just as it is in a small submarine. There are two chemical carbon dioxide scrubbers that will extract CO_2 from the air. You'll need to bleed oxygen from the cylinders at regular intervals to maintain the air pressure." Buxton indicated a pressure gauge on one of the walls.

None of them mentioned what would happen when the oxygen finally ran out. Then they'd have to breathe the outside air, and the only thing between them and fungal infection would be the unproven Megacrine drug.

The compartment also contained a barely concealed chemical toilet. There were no cooking facilities, but plenty of concentrated and canned foods. And a large tank of drinking water.

Next to three bulky anti-contamination suits that hung from the roof was a row of weapons. Four 7.62mm FNL1 rifles, two Sterling L2A3 submachine guns, and two Smith & Wesson .38 revolvers.

"We're packing a lot of firepower," Slocock observed. "All these and those two guns on the roof."

"A 7.62mm machine gun on this roof and a 7.62mm GEC minigun mount on the roof of the driver's cabin. Both are remote-controlled from inside the cabin. The only drawback with them is that you'll have to go outside to refill their ammunition boxes. And I'm afraid you'll also have to go outside if you have a need to use this."

Buxton bent down and opened up a long metal box that was lying across several cases of 7.62mm ammunition. Slocock whistled. Inside the case was a Breda NATO-issue antitank gun. "You're familiar with the weapon, I trust, Sergeant?"

Slocock nodded. "How many rockets?"

"Six." Buxton touched an ammunition case with the toe of his boot. "In there. They each contain a pin-stabilized hollow charge round which can penetrate 320mm of armor plating at 0 degree incidence, and 120mm at 65 degrees incidence. Effective range is approximately 600 meters."

Wilson said, in astonishment, "Why on earth do we need something like that? I thought our only danger, apart from the fungus itself, was from angry mobs of infected people."

"Dr. Wilson, an awful lot of people have been cut off inside the quarantine area, including a number of military units. We know for certain that some members of these units have mutinied. On several occasions to date soldiers have attempted to break out through the quarantine barrier using their equipment. The result has been pitched battles between them and units outside the quarantine area. So far, we've kept them in."

Wilson looked grim. "You're saying we may have to fight our way through fully armed groups of soldiers? This whole thing gets more and more hopeless with each passing moment."

"Hopefully you'll be able to avoid any such confrontations. The beauty of the Stalwart here is that it can go practically anywhere, including through rivers and canals. If you should spot any army vehicles ahead of you, just try to detour around them," said Buxton.

"Yeah, *easy*," muttered Slocock.

"There are also two portable flame-throwers in a locked container clamped to the rear of the vehicle. Not enough room for them in here, besides they'd stink the place out. Your air systems wouldn't be able to cope. But they may come in handy when you reach London. I hear the fungus can grow pretty thick in places." He looked at his watch. "I suggest you get moving at first light, which is less than four hours away.

"Sergeant Slocock, I'll have one of my engineers give you a run-through on all the equipment so you can familiarize yourself with it."

"No need, sir," said Slocock quickly, anxious to hit the sack with his bottle. "I'll pick it up along the way."

Buxton gave him an expressionless look. He said quietly, "I think it would be a good idea to have the run-through, Sergeant. The automatic gun controls are especially tricky."

The Major's tone of voice told Slocock it would be a waste of time arguing. Besides, he didn't have the strength. "Yessir."

Buxton turned to Wilson. "As for you, Doctor, you might as well get some shut-eye."

"All right, but first I want to check in on Kimberley."

"Yeah, you do that, Doctor," said Slocock with a barely concealed sneer. "And while you're at it take her temperature for me too."

"That's enough, Sergeant," said Buxton curtly. "Stay here. I'll send Sergeant Boardman along. He helped customize this beast so he can tell you everything you need to know. And I'd appreciate it if you didn't touch another drop of what's in your kitbag. Understand?"

When the Major and Wilson had gone Slocock slumped onto the bunk and pulled the bottle out of his bag. He took a long drink and frowned as he thought about Wilson. He'd been clucking around Kimberley like a bloody mother hen ever since they'd left Bangor. And she, the bitch, seemed to be lapping it up. Well, he'd put a stop to that somehow . . .

"I hope you won't have any trouble with him," said Major Buxton as they left the shed.

Wilson glanced at the young, serious-faced officer. "With Slocock? Should I?"

"I've been talking to his commanding officer in Belfast. The Sergeant's a good soldier in many ways but he has a record for being a trouble-maker. And there were certain incidents involving him that were under investigation . . ."

"Incidents?"

"Shootings. On three occasions he has shot and killed men, while on patrol, who he claimed were carrying firearms. A gun was found on only one of them. Apparently the other two men had no connection with the IRA. And as all three incidents happened in a relatively short space of time it suggests that the Sergeant has become, how shall we put it . . . ?"

"Trigger happy?"

"I'm afraid so. Not the sort of chap I'd personally have picked for a job like this."

"But I understand he volunteered."

"Yes. Which is rather worrying, don't you think?"

Wilson found Kimberley running a checklist on her medical supplies and equipment which she'd laid out on her bunk in the empty barrack room. She was looking a little better but was still shockingly white and her army-issue t-shirt was soaked with sweat despite the coolness of the night.

"Almost time for us to have our shots," she said. "Where's the Sergeant?"

"Still outside, playing with his battle-wagon." He then told her what Buxton had said about Slocock. She didn't seem alarmed.

"Someone who shoots first and asks questions later is the sort of man this situation calls for. The Major's living in the past. What does he think his men are doing out there at this very minute?"

She was referring to the gunfire that had been going on in the distance ever since they'd arrived. The camp was close to the barrier. The troops strung out along it were continually shooting at refugees who were trying to escape from the ever-growing infected area. Even so Wilson was a little chilled by the callousness of her words. It revealed an aspect of her that he hadn't suspected existed.

"But the Major has a point in wondering why Slocock volunteered for this job. I mean, what man in his right mind would?"

She gave him a weary smile. "You did."

"No. I had no choice. I was drafted. But Slocock . . ." A thought struck him. "And *you*. You volunteered. You know our chances of surviving until they find the means of eradicating the plague are pretty slim, so why are you throwing your life away?"

She shrugged. "I want to see the fungus stopped and destroyed. It's as simple as that."

Is it? he wondered.

They got underway at 5.45 a.m. They were escorted to the barrier by Major Buxton in a Saracen armored car. The barrier consisted of great rolls of barbed wire that stretched off into the distance in both directions. Behind the wire, small groups of soldiers were positioned at regular intervals, backed up by the occasional armored vehicle. There was a gap in the wire where it crossed the road. Two tanks sat in the middle of the road, plugging the gap. They began to trundle to the side as the Stalwart approached.

The Saracen also pulled up on the side of the road.

The opening between the two tanks yawned like the mouth of some monster. *Abandon hope all ye who enter here*, Wilson thought grimly.

"Well, cheerio chaps," came Buxton's unnaturally jovial voice over the radio. "This is as far as I go. But I'll be with you in spirit all the way."

"You have no idea what that means to me, sir," said Slocock into the mike.

Buxton ignored the sarcasm. "Don't forget to report in on this frequency at half-hourly intervals or in the event of emergencies. Goodbye and good luck."

"Well, here goes nothing," said Slocock. He took a swallow from the bottle sitting between his legs and then gunned the engine. The Stalwart lurched forward and sped through the gap.

12

"It's a beautiful day," said Wilson, peering up at the cloudless blue sky.

"Keep your eyes on the bloody road," growled Slocock.

They'd been traveling for over half an hour now and even though Slocock intended doing most, if not all, of the driving he thought it would be wise if Wilson knew the basics of handling the Stalwart. He'd even instructed Wilson on how to operate the guns, despite his insistence that he could never bring himself to use them.

They were heading down the A449 towards Worcester in order to avoid the chaos that was apparently surrounding Birmingham and Coventry. North of Worcester they would try and get onto the M5, if it was clear, and proceed toward Gloucester, then across on the A40 and M40 to London, making a wide detour around Oxford as well.

Everything looked deceptively normal, apart from the lack of traffic on the road. So far their worst moments had come during the first few miles on the other side of the barricade. They had seen the first of the bodies almost immediately. They were everywhere; lying across the road; hanging half out of their bullet-riddled cars; huddled together in groups beside the road.

At first Slocock tried to avoid running over them. But it was impossible, so he stopped trying. Wilson shuddered every time he felt the tires go over something.

The bodies nearest the wire were all badly charred.

"Flamethrowers," said Slocock. "To kill the fungus. A fucking lot of good it does."

But so far Wilson hadn't seen a sign of the fungus on any of the bodies they'd passed.

A half-mile past the barrier, they entered the "dead zone," as Slocock called it. It was a total wasteland in which nothing lived. Parts of it were blackened and burned; other parts were covered in a strange white powder. At one point they saw a plane flying low across the ground to their east, leaving a trail of yellow dust behind it. Later they saw, in the distance, a jet dropping napalm.

They passed several burned-out vehicles, their occupants charred husks with rictus grins, their teeth showing white against their blackened flesh.

On these occasions Wilson was glad Kimberley wasn't sitting up front with them. The motion of the truck made her feel even sicker and she'd gone to lie on one of the bunks even before they'd reached the barrier.

Both men felt uneasy as they drove through the "dead zone." They knew that the Air Force had been informed of their crossing, but this was no guarantee that some pilot might not decide to attack them, either for the sheer hell of it or because he hadn't received the message about them.

Slocock pushed his foot down. But speed was dangerous on the battered road surface, and there were several sections where the road disappeared completely—obliterated by massive bomb craters. Slocock was obliged to slow down and drive off the road around them.

Finally they saw green ahead of them and knew they were almost out of the man-made wilderness.

On the other side of the zone they passed a large group of disconsolate-looking people sitting beside a number of parked cars. They'd obviously decided not to risk trying to cross the zone, or perhaps had heard from fleeing survivors what was waiting for them even if they got through.

Most of them just stared apathetically at the speeding Stalwart; a few looked puzzled at the fact it was traveling in the wrong direction, and a few raised their fists angrily at this symbol of the now-hated military. None of them, Wilson saw, displayed any external sign of fungal infection.

When the road ahead seemed clear and undamaged, Slocock suggested, or rather ordered, that Wilson take a turn behind the wheel.

Wilson drove for about 10 minutes and was almost beginning to enjoy himself, absurd as that seemed in the circumstances.

"Okay, that's enough," said Slocock suddenly. "Pull up and I'll take over. We're getting near Kidderminster."

As Wilson crawled over Slocock, he decided to check on Kimberley. He was tempted to go through the heavy hatch that separated the driver's cabin from the rear compartment, but undoing the seals was a difficult business so he flipped the intercom switch instead. "Hi, Kimberley! How are you doing?"

There was a long pause before she answered, rather irritably, "I was asleep."

"Oh." He glanced at Slocock and saw the expected sneer. "Sorry. Are you feeling any better?"

"No. Where are we?"

He told her they were approaching Kidderminster. She said she was going back to sleep and not to wake her unless something important happened. He switched off the intercom with a sigh.

They rode on in silence for a while. Then Wilson pointed at the bottle of whiskey resting upright against Slocock's crotch like a glass phallus. "Mind if I have a drink?"

"Piss off," said Slocock.

Wilson wondered if he was joking.

"Does that mean no?"

"Look mate, I've only got another four bottles left."

"That's plenty."

"Not the way I drink. And who knows how long it's going to be before I get my hands on any more. So I'm sure as hell not wasting any of it on you."

"You don't like me very much, do you?"

Slocock laughed. "You intellectuals are real sharp. Yeah, you're right. I don't like you. My job is to make sure you stay alive long enough to do *your* job. After that, well, we'll see."

Wilson realized, with a mild shock, that Slocock was making some kind of threat. And yet he was surprised to note that it didn't particularly disturb him. There were too many other things to worry about.

"Well, as Flannery would say in a situation like this, 'Up yours, boyo.'"

Slocock grunted. "Who the fuck's Flannery?"

"An old friend of mine."

"Sounds like a real wit. But whoever he is he's too far away to do you any good."

"You're wrong there. He's closer than you think," said Wilson and smiled.

They made a wide detour around Kidderminster just to be safe even though the town appeared deserted. Slocock sent the Stalwart off the road, through a fence and across the fields.

Wilson winced when the vehicle crushed the fence under its tires. "Aren't you afraid we might get a flat? I noticed we're not carrying a spare."

"They're puncture-proof. The tubes are honey-combed with lots of separate cells inflated with nitrogen."

They got back on the A449 without any difficulty and were heading south toward Worcester when they encountered a group of nine people coming along the road. Five men, two women, and two young children. Wilson expected Slocock to speed by them as he had the other group, but to his surprise the Stalwart began to slow down.

"Why are you stopping?"

"Take a closer look at them."

As the truck came to a halt about 20 yards from the group Wilson saw what Slocock was talking about.

They were victims of the fungus.

Compared with Dr. Bruce Carter on the video they seemed scarcely affected, but it was there nonetheless. They all appeared to be subject to a particularly dark blue five o'clock shadow. The women and children too. And the same blue coloring was on their hands as well.

Wilson felt his flesh crawl.

The group had come to a halt and were staring silently at the vehicle. They projected a sense of hopeless despair.

"Can't we do anything at all for them?" Wilson asked Slocock.

"Yeah, we could shoot the poor bastards."

Wilson didn't take him seriously until he reached up and pulled down one of the folding gun-control units from the ceiling of the cabin.

"No!" cried Wilson, grabbing his arm. "Don't! Let them live!"

"Why? They're finished anyway. If they get through the dead zone they'll die on Buxton's barrier. Be doing them a favor to put them out of their misery right now."

"And I say let them be!" cried Wilson, his voice rising to a shout.

Slocock shrugged and said, "Okay, don't get excited." He started the truck moving again. "Your trouble, mate, is that you're too squeamish. But you won't be for long."

As Slocock drove past the group Wilson got a closer look at the blue mold covering their faces and hands. He avoided looking at their eyes.

They stood motionless as the truck went by. Not much more than two weeks ago, Wilson realized, these had been normal, healthy people. But now, thanks to one mistake made in a laboratory in distant London, their world had been turned upside down and destroyed almost overnight. And he too was doomed . . .

Later, as they got nearer to Worcester, Wilson began to notice streaks of color that were alien to a British summer landscape. Bright orange, purple, blue and red . . . they were not the color of flowers; the orange was brighter than marigolds and seemed to glow unhealthily, and the purple suggested something that was rotting rather than living. Worse were the large patches of gray. On one occasion they passed an entire field of grayness. Whatever the crop was—either wheat or barley—it was covered with a thick coating of gray fuzz.

"Well, we're in the land of the magic mushroom for sure now," said Slocock and took another drink from his bottle.

The sight made Wilson aware that the fungus attacked other living things apart from people. Crops and livestock right across England were being destroyed, which meant there would be a tremendous food shortage in the months ahead. Those who survived the fungus would most probably die of starvation.

Ahead of them, where Worcester lay, they saw columns of smoke rising into the sky. "Looks as if someone's torched the place," said Slocock. Then, a short distance further along, he brought the truck to a halt and snatched up a pair of powerful binoculars.

"What is it?" asked Wilson. He could see some moving dots in the distance but couldn't make them out.

"Army convoy. Four trucks. Two tanks in the lead. New 'Challenger' tanks. Must be planning to try and break through the barrier. And they have a good chance of succeeding with those babies. They carry Chobham armor."

"Are you going to make contact with them? They might be able to give us information about conditions between here and London."

"They're just as likely to blow us to small pieces. I'm going to give them as wide a berth as possible." Again he drove the Stalwart off the road and into a field. "This is going to slow us up but I don't want to take chances at this stage of the game."

As the vehicle bounced over the rough ground the intercom buzzed. Wilson pressed the switch and heard Kimberley ask worriedly what was happening.

"Nothing. Just a little detour. Go back to bed," he answered.

"I just fell *out* of bed. It's like being in a barrel going over Niagara Falls back here. I'm coming through."

"Shit," muttered Slocock.

Wilson helped her open the small, circular hatch and then assisted her through it. She came feet first and he supported her legs until she was all the way through. She landed on the seat between them with a thump. "Thanks," she said. She smelled of sweat but it was a smell Wilson didn't mind. And he saw she was looking much better. Still pale, but more like her old self.

"I don't think it's a good idea for all three of us to be up front at once," growled Slocock. "If the cabin gets holed or we break a window, we all get exposed."

"And if that happened what good would it do having me sealed off in that tin can?" said Kimberley. "I'd be helpless."

"But still pure and untouched, Doctor," said Slocock, giving her a suggestive grin. "And there'd be a lot you could do. Like climb into one of the suits and bring the other two to us. They wouldn't do *us* any good, of course, but at least we could keep our contamination away from you."

Wilson tapped the thick glass of the narrow windshield with his knuckle and said worriedly, "I thought you said this was special armored glass, bullet-proof and all that."

"It is. Doesn't mean it'll stop everything though."

Kimberley was peering round at the passing scenery. "Where the hell are we?"

"According to the map this is Fernhill Heath. I'm cutting across it toward the M5," said Slocock.

"We saw an army convoy coming toward us," explained Wilson. "And the sergeant thought it would be a good idea to avoid them."

Kimberley said, "Well, don't look now, but isn't that another bunch of soldiers right in front of us?"

"Shit, she's right!" cried Slocock, slowing down.

Wilson looked and saw a line of armed men appearing out of a row of trees ahead of them. He hadn't spotted them earlier because they were wearing camouflage. Several of them were waving as they approached.

Slocock stopped the truck and sat there drumming his fingers nervously on the steering wheel. "I don't like this. There are over 30 of them and some are packing anti-tank weapons. They could take us out no trouble."

"Why should they want to?" asked Wilson. "They're army, and this is an army vehicle. They're not to know we're from outside."

"Maybe," said Slocock edgily.

The main body of men came to a stop some 50 feet from the Stalwart, but four of them kept coming.

As they came closer Wilson experienced a sudden *frisson*. What he had thought was camouflage paint on their uniforms, faces and hands was, in fact, fungus. They weren't *wearing* any uniforms. Instead their bodies were coated in a tortoise-shell pattern of green, brown, black and yellow patches of mold.

"Good God," said Kimberley softly.

The four men, waving as they came, were now less than 20 feet away. One of them was shouting something, but as the cabin was airtight they couldn't make out what he was saying. When Slocock shook his head to show he didn't understand the man then pantomined that they should come out of the truck. He appeared to be grinning but the coloring on his face made it hard to tell.

Slocock muttered, "Balls to that," and shook his head again.

The four men promptly dropped to the ground and aimed their weapons. At the same moment the row of men behind them started firing. There were several sharp *pinging* noises as bullets struck the Stalwart's armor plating and, to Wilson's horror, two white smears appeared on the windshield. He ducked down on his seat, expecting the glass to shatter at any second.

Slocock quickly pulled down one of the gun controls and pressed the red firing button. On the cabin roof the GEC minigun began to make a sound like a sewing machine.

Spurts of soil were kicked up around the four nearest men. Suddenly all four of them were writhing on the ground as the minigun hosed them with high velocity bullets.

"Get the other gun firing, quickly!" yelled Slocock.

Unwillingly, Wilson reached up and pulled down the control unit for the big 7.62mm machine gun. The unit was like a smaller version of a submarine periscope. It had two handles on either side. Rotating them up or down controlled the gun's elevation and turning the whole unit made the turret swivel correspondingly. There was even an eyepiece linked to a sight on the gun by flexible fiber optics.

Wilson looked through the eyepiece and got a close-up view of part of the ragged line of men shooting at them.

"Fire, you asshole, fire!" Slocock bellowed. "Before they start using their heavy stuff on us!"

Slocock was now directing the stream of fire from the high-speed minigun at the other men. Two of them immediately fell but bullets were still hitting the track at an alarming rate. They made a sound like a rain of large hailstones.

Wilson had his thumb on the red firing button but couldn't bring himself to press it. Then he heard the minigun stop.

"Christ, I'm out of ammo! *Shoot*, damn you, Wilson!"

But he still couldn't press the button.

The next thing Wilson knew he'd been shoved roughly aside as Slocock leaned over Kimberley and snatched the gun control away from him.

Then the big machine gun opened up.

In the distance Wilson saw the bodies of several of the mold-covered men jerk and twist as the bullets slammed into them. The others started to retreat back toward the row of trees.

Slocock kept firing, spraying bullets back and forth along the fleeing line of men. More of them fell. Soon none of them were on their feet. Several lay writhing with agony on the ground, while a few were trying to drag themselves toward the cover of the trees.

Slocock kept firing.

Wilson turned to tell him to stop but saw the expression on his face and said nothing.

Even when all the bodies were motionless Slocock kept shooting. He didn't stop until the gun ran out of ammunition.

Wilson knew now why Slocock had volunteered for the mission.

13

"You stupid bastard! You almost got us all killed! The next time I tell you to shoot, you *shoot*, understand!" Slocock was shaking with anger and looked as if he could easily add Wilson to the pile of bodies in front of the truck.

Wilson was trembling himself, though whether from fear, shock, or simple disgust he didn't know. "I'm sorry," he muttered, "But I'm not used to machine-gunning people down. I haven't had your practice at it."

Slocock's eyes narrowed. There was a pause and then he said, in a quieter voice, "Well, matey, you'd better learn pretty quick-smartish if you want to stay alive."

Wilson glanced at Kimberley for support but she was staring straight ahead, her expression dazed.

"Are you okay?" he asked her.

She nodded, then turned to Slocock. "Why do you think they attacked us?"

"Guess they wanted the vehicle. Or maybe the food supplies we're carrying. But whatever they wanted, it stopped them from using their anti-tank gear, until it was too late." He shot Wilson another accusing look.

Wilson turned his attention to the windshield. He pointed to one of the starry smears. "You think that's cracked all the way through?"

"Nah. Just the outer layer by the look of it. We were lucky." He twisted round and began to unseal the hatch. "I'm going to suit up and go reload the ammunition boxes. I'll do a damage check as well while I'm out there."

When Slocock had shut the hatch behind him Wilson said to Kimberley, "What are we going to do about him?"

She didn't answer for a time. Then she said, "He's right, you know. You did almost get us killed."

He looked at her in amazement. "Are you serious? You're taking *his* side on this? Kimberley, the man is a psychopath! I told you what Buxton said about him and this proves it."

"Whatever he is, he saved our lives just then. He's our only chance of making it to London. We need him."

"You're condoning mass murder?"

"It was self-defense. Besides, too much is at stake for us to be overly sensitive about the lives of a few people who were doomed anyway."

"That's a fine way for a doctor to talk."

She sighed. "Don't be naive. We're doing this for the greater good, remember?"

He was about to continue arguing when a red light began to flash on the radio. Wilson pressed the "receive" switch and heard Slocock saying, via his suit radio, "I'm outside now. Just about to climb onto the roof. Keep your eyes peeled for any sign of movement. Give me a yell if you see as much as a leaf fall."

They both listened to the sounds of Slocock clambering over the roof. Ahead of the truck all was still. Wilson was relieved to see that none of the bodies scattered about showed any sign of life.

Slocock finished reloading the guns, then climbed back down and came around to the front of the vehicle. They watched as the bulky white anti-contamination suit disappeared from view as Slocock bent down to peer under the truck.

Then they heard him say over the radio, "One of you start the engine, will you."

Wilson was going to crawl past Kimberley but she said, "I'll do it," and slid into the driver's seat. She switched on the ignition. The engine made a wheezing sound but didn't start. "What's wrong?" she asked Slocock.

"Dunno," came his reply over the radio. "We got three bloody holes here. Some bastard was firing armor piercing bullets. And there's a great puddle of oil under the engine."

"You mean we're stuck here?" asked Wilson, alarmed.

"Don't know until I look at the damage. We've got spare parts and tools—might be able to fix it. But this armor cowling is going to be hell to get off."

"Shit," said Wilson. The thought of having to walk all the way to London filled him with despair. It would take days. And they'd never be able to do it wearing the anti-contamination suits.

"You any good with cars, Wilson?" asked Slocock. "I'm going to need some help out here."

"No. I'm useless at anything mechanical. Can't even change a typewriter ribbon without . . ."

"I'll help you," Kimberley told Slocock. "Where I come from, if you can't fix your own car when it breaks down, it stays where it is for keeps."

"Good girl. Put a suit on and get out here pronto. And bring the tool box with you. As for you, Wilson, the guns are loaded again now. If you see anything coming our way you *shoot*, understand?"

"Yes. I understand," said Wilson grudgingly.

As Kimberley opened the hatch and prepared to crawl through he said to her, "Be careful out there."

She grimaced. "Oh, come *on*, Barry. Save the clichés for your books."

Deeply stung, he was at a loss for words as she disappeared through the hatch and swung it shut behind her.

He sat there fuming with anger for about an hour while Kimberley donned one of the suits and joined Slocock at the front of the truck. For a time he listened in on their conversation, but he got bored with their talk about past experiences with the internal combustion engine as they struggled to remove the cowling, and he switched off the radio.

It was hot in the cab and getting hotter. There was no air-conditioning, only a vent leading from the rear compartment which could be instantly sealed in an emergency. Wilson decided to leave the hatch open for a while to let what air there was circulate better.

At 11.30 a.m. Slocock and Kimberley returned for something to eat and drink. Wilson joined them in the rear section and helped them out of their suits, which stank of disinfectant.

"How bad is the damage?" he asked.

Slocock collapsed on one of the bunks and wiped the sweat from his face, which was glowing red from the heat and the exertion.

"Pretty bad. We're leaking oil like a sieve and the fuel pump's out of commission. Radiator's also got a hole in it, but that's the least of our problems."

"Can it be fixed?"

"We can do some temporary repairs. Fuel pump's going to be a real pisser. Whether it'll get us to London is anyone's guess."

"How long will it take you to fix things?"

Slocock shrugged and looked at Kimberley. She said, "At least another four hours. Possibly longer."

"We'll never reach London by tonight."

"No," agreed Slocock. "We'll have to stop for the night somewhere along the way. I don't feel like driving this around in the darkness with things the way they are out there."

An atmosphere of gloom settled over them as they shared

a thermos of coffee, provided by their Wolverhampton army hosts, and ate a can each of cold stew.

Then, after Kimberley had given them their shots of Megacrine, the two of them got into their suits again while Wilson returned to his vigil in the driver's cab.

Before Slocock left, Wilson asked him whether they should report to Buxton and tell him what had happened. Slocock vetoed the idea. "Screw Buxton. Why waste time talking to him or anyone else on the outside? They can't help us. When we've got some information for them we'll send it, but until then they can sweat it out. Serves 'em right."

It was even hotter in the cab now, and Wilson was quickly drenched in sweat.

Wearily he made periodic sweeps of the area with the binoculars, but all remained still.

Then, while making one of these sweeps, he noticed something odd. He happened to focus on one of the bodies lying in the distance and saw that it had undergone some kind of change.

The fungus covering it had grown thicker. It was now almost impossible to tell that there was a man's corpse under it.

Puzzled, Wilson investigated the four bodies lying closer to the truck. They too had changed. They now looked as if they were covered by patchwork fur blankets.

He switched on the radio and drew his companions' attention to the phenomenon. They'd been too busy to notice what was happening, but now one of the white-suited figures walked over to the nearest corpse and kneeled next to it.

He heard Kimberley's voice say, "Fascinating. The fungus seems to have mutated. Now that the host is dead, it's changed from being a parasite into a saprophyte."

He winced as he saw her reach out and touch the growth.

"For God's sake, be careful!" he called.

"Relax. It can't hurt me. You should see this, Barry. The rate of tissue absorption is remarkable. There's hardly anything left of this man apart from his bones."

Slocock's voice suddenly boomed out of the radio. "Kim, stop messing around and get back to work. You'll have more than enough time to look at fungi when we reach London."

Wilson was relieved when Kimberley's white-suited form left the man-shaped mound and returned to the front of the truck.

The day wore on. Slocock and Kimberley took another break, then went back to work. Conditions in the suits were almost intolerable, they told Wilson. Apart from the heat, the visibility was frustratingly poor as the face-plates kept misting up. Equally frustrating was trying to do anything delicate with the thick gloves. And there was also the constant fear they would puncture or rip the suits.

By four in the afternoon Wilson was struggling to keep awake in the stuffy, overheated cab. He'd made two trips that afternoon to the rear compartment to bleed more oxygen into the air, but it didn't seem to improve things.

He was just starting to nod off again when he spotted movement in the trees ahead of the truck. Jolted into full awareness he reached up for the controls of the big machine gun.

Through the sight he got a glimpse of something monstrous coming straight toward the truck. It was moving on four legs and was very large. Its head was massive and bulbous and it seemed to be covered in thick, green strands that hung from it like clumps of seaweed.

Wilson pressed the firing button. He was off-target to begin with but quickly compensated and proceeded to spray the monster with high-velocity bullets.

The thing shuddered and its front legs collapsed beneath it. It skidded forward for about three yards then lay there kicking. Wilson continued to pour bullets into it.

"Okay, Wilson, it's dead!" came Slocock's shout over the radio. "Stop wasting ammunition!"

Wilson took his finger off the button and took a deep breath. He was, he realized, shaking. "What the hell is that thing?"

Slocock and Kimberley walked over to the creature. After a long pause Slocock laughed and said, "Congratulations, Wilson. You've just killed a cow."

"A cow?" Wilson couldn't believe the ghastly apparition was nothing more than a cow.

"Poor bitch must have been driven crazy by the stuff growing on her. Next time, Eagle-eye, don't waste so many bullets."

Wilson's brief feeling of satisfaction evaporated. For a moment he'd thought he'd saved both their lives. Now, he felt foolish. Slocock was laughing at him and so, he suspected, was Kimberley.

They didn't finish working on the engine until after 7 p.m. When they came back inside and stripped off their suits they both looked exhausted.

"God, I stink," said Kimberley, sniffing at her sweat-stained t-shirt. "I'd give anything for a shower. Or even a wash."

Wilson couldn't prevent himself from staring at the clear outline of her breasts through the damp material. The nipples were plainly visible. He felt a rush of desire for her and wished, yet again, that Slocock wasn't around.

"Can't spare the water," grunted Slocock, "you'll just have to keep stinking."

"How's the engine?" asked Wilson.

Slocock shrugged. "A 50/50 chance it'll get us to London. But I'm not doing any driving tonight. I'm too tired. I'll park the bus under those trees to give us some cover, and then I think we should turn in. We'll make an early start in the morning."

After Slocock had driven the truck into the shelter of the trees, they had an unexciting meal of more cold stew, fruit salad, and bars of chocolate. Then Kimberley gave them their shots and they prepared for bed.

"Kim and I will take the bunks," said Slocock as he stretched out on one of them. "We did all the work. All you did was play Buffalo Bill."

Surprised, Wilson was about to protest but there was nothing he could say that wouldn't make him appear ridiculous. He looked helplessly at Kimberley but she seemed completely unconcerned by Slocock's declaration. She lay back on the other bunk and closed her eyes.

Forcing himself to sound casual, Wilson said, "Okay, I'll sleep in the cab."

"You don't sleep, Eagle-eye, you keep watch," Wilson told him. "You can sleep back here when we get moving in the morning."

Anger flared up in Wilson but he held himself in check. The

trouble was, Slocock was right. One of them should stay on guard and it was obvious that he was the most rested. So he simply muttered goodnight and made his way forward. Kimberley already appeared to be asleep.

"Don't slam the door on your way out," said Slocock, and sniggered.

Wilson sat alone in the cab feeling absurdly jealous. He was certain—almost certain—he had nothing to be jealous about, but the small amount of doubt was sufficient to make him acutely uncomfortable.

He told himself it was inconceivable that Kimberley would let herself be touched by Slocock. He had seen the antagonism between them.

And yet this evening the antagonism seemed to have vanished altogether. And he remembered how she'd defended Slocock after the shooting incident that morning.

And they'd been working together all afternoon . . .

And he called her "Kim" now . . .

Wilson lasted for an hour and then, hating himself, he switched on the intercom.

Immediately he heard a cry from Kimberley. It sounded like a cry of pain.

Christ, Slocock's raping her!

But before he could leap up and go to her aid he realized the true nature of her cries. It wasn't rape. On the contrary.

Wilson sat there frozen. He didn't want to listen. Each sound she made cut through him like a hot knife. But he couldn't switch the intercom off.

"Oh, God . . . *yes* . . . harder . . . harder . . . come on, *hurt* me . . . *harder* . . . yes . . . ohhhhh . . ." Her voice rose almost to a scream.

Wilson felt like screaming himself.

They lay limply entwined on Slocock's bunk, their bodies covered in a sheen of sweat. They were both breathing heavily. Slocock figured they must have used up half a cylinder of oxygen with their exertions. Still, it had been worth it. Hell, yes.

"Hey, Doc, you know you had a pretty rare experience tonight," he told her.

She half-opened her eyes and looked at him drowsily. "Well, I'll admit it was good, but it was far from rare."

"I meant me. That." He pointed at his penis which lay, still tumescent, against his right thigh. "First time I've managed to get it up in ages."

Her eyes widened with surprise. "Seriously?"

He nodded. "Yeah. One of the reasons Marge—my wife—left me. The main reason actually." He didn't mind talking about it to her. He felt too pleased with himself to care.

"So how come you were able to just then?"

"Partly you, I guess. And the situation. The excitement . . . first time in a long time I've felt really alive."

"You mean you find being in danger a turn-on?"

"Something like that."

"You're full of surprises, Sergeant."

"So are you, Doctor." It had been she who'd made the first move. He'd woken up to find her standing naked beside his bunk. "I didn't think I was your type. And I didn't figure you for the type who liked it rough."

"In a way I'm like you. I like to feel threatened. I like men who scare me. But the men I know wouldn't really harm me."

"You want to feel safe and threatened at the same time?"

"You could put it that way."

"I know where I'd like to put it." He took her hand and placed it on his penis which was becoming fully erect again. "How can you be sure I won't hurt you for real?"

"I'm 90 percent sure. The other 10 percent is what makes it exciting."

He was thoughtful for a while, then said, "Know what I'm going to do to you?"

"No. Tell me."

He told her at great length and in great clinical detail. When he'd finished she nodded. She said, "In my medical bag over there you'll find a jar of vaseline. Make sure you use a lot of it."

Wilson kept listening, still unable to press the switch. His imagination created images to match the sounds that were probably even more outrageous than the reality.

The sound both infuriated him and aroused him to an intolerable level. Eventually they stopped. There was silence for a time and then Slocock started to snore.

Wilson switched off the intercom. And sat staring off into the blackness of the night.

14

Slocock was back in Belfast.

He and his unit were in the Falls Road. They were in full anti-riot gear. Behind them, as back-up, was a Saracen armored car. In front of them was a mob. Kids, mainly, and a few young men. All of them were heaving stones, half-bricks and chunks of pavement.

The rain of missiles was so dense that the sound they made hitting the armored Saracen was deafening. Occasionally one of the men would receive a direct hit and, despite the protection of his helmet, have to be helped away towards the rear of the army lines.

As Slocock watched the taunting mob through his transparent riot shield he itched to have the freedom simply to open up with his rifle.

A different type of missile came hurtling out of the crowd. Slocock glimpsed it as it arced overhead. He saw the red sparks and his bowels went icy cold.

A gasoline bomb.

He had a fear of fire. It was his big weakness.

Paralyzed with terror, he couldn't move as the bottle shattered in the road right in front of him. The blazing liquid showered over him, setting him alight. He screamed. He woke up trying to beat out the flames engulfing his body. Then he realized he was naked and lying on his bunk.

But he could still hear the stones hitting the armored car!

As he sat up in alarm the light came on. Kimberley, still naked, stared at him with shocked eyes. "What's happening?"

"I don't know." He grabbed for his pants and started to pull them on.

The hatchway was opening. Wilson's startled face appeared. If it was surprised at seeing Kimberley naked he didn't show it. "We must be surrounded!" he cried. "We're being hit from every direction at once, but I can't see anyone out there!"

Slocock ran to the hatchway, pushed Wilson out of the way, and slid through into the cab. He saw that Wilson had turned the headlights on, and a large area ahead of the truck was clearly illuminated. But there was no one in sight.

And yet even as he peered out he could see numerous round objects hurtling between the trees towards them. The clatter as the things hit the roof and sides of the vehicle was continuous. Then one of them hit the windshield. Immediately there was a large red stain spreading across the glass. A second one hit the windshield, then a third. The stain got bigger.

"Fruit! They're throwing bloody fruit at us!" said Slocock.

He started firing the minigun, spraying bullets indiscriminately. But the barrage of brown, orange-like objects didn't lessen.

When the gun was empty he switched to the other one.

"Can't we just drive the hell away from this?" cried Wilson.

That's what we should have done, Slocock thought bitterly, cursing himself, but now it was too late. He pointed at the windshield. It was almost completely obscured. "We'd probably drive straight into a tree and be stuck here for good."

The big gun chattered on until it too was empty. Slocock had swept it back and forth round a full 360 degrees. He must have hit *some* of them out there but the barrage was as heavy as ever. He was stumped.

Wilson, on the other hand, had suddenly started to smile. He had been staring hard at the stuff on the windshield and then his face had lit up. He turned to Slocock. "I'm going out there."

"Are you crazy? There must be an army of them."

Wilson continued to smile his annoying smile and said, "An army, yes. But not of people. There are no people out there at all."

"What the bloody hell are you talking about?"

But Wilson refused to say anything else. Slocock, mystified, had no choice but to follow Wilson into the rear section. There Kimberley, now dressed, asked them what was going on.

"We got a couple of hundred people out there chucking balls full of red gunge at us but Buffalo Bill here claims it's all an illusion."

Wilson was climbing into one of the suits. Before he put on the helmet he said, "Coming, Sergeant, or are you going to cower in here for the rest of the night?"

Reluctantly Slocock suited up as well. He picked up one of the rifles from the rack but Wilson shook his head. "You won't need it."

"I'll be the judge of that," he said as he checked to see that the magazine was full.

Wilson went out through the airlock first, carrying just a powerful flashlight.

When Slocock warily emerged from the rear hatch he saw Wilson some distance away aiming the flashlight beam at something on the ground.

Almost immediately Slocock felt a sharp impact on his stomach. He grunted and doubled over, winded.

"Move away from the truck!" came Wilson's voice over the suit radio. "I think it's the heat that attracts them. And protect your face-plate. One of these things could easily crack it open!"

Still bent over, and covering his face-plate with his free hand, Slocock staggered over to where Wilson was standing.

"Look!" he cried, pointing at the ground.

Slocock looked and saw that the ground between the trees was covered with a thick yellow carpet. Suddenly he saw a movement in the thick growth and got a blurred glimpse of one of the round missiles shooting upwards out of the stuff. Then he saw another . . . and another.

"What *is* it?" he demanded.

"*Sphaerobolus,*" said Wilson with a crazy kind of glee in his voice. Slocock wondered if he was starting to crack.

"It's a fungus where the fruit body acts as a catapult," explained Wilson happily. "Inside the fruit body there's a tiny sphere called a gleba, except in this case it's not so tiny. On average these specimens must measure five inches across." He ducked as one of the round missiles shot by him. "The gleba floats in a sort of rotting fluid. The pressure builds up in the fruit body as it matures and then eventually an inner wall suddenly turns inside-out and flicks the gleba away. An ordinary gleba can be ejected over a distance of several yards, but these are traveling over 10 times that. It's incredible!"

"Fuck incredible." Slocock aimed the rifle and fired a series of shots into the yellow fungus. Then he waded into the stuff, which came up to his knees, and started using the weapon as a club. Liquid popping sounds could be heard as Slocock's frenzied assault sent up shreds and particles of the yellow growth into the air.

"You're wasting your time, Slocock! There's too much of it! There's nothing we can do!" called Wilson.

Slocock quickly exhausted himself and allowed Wilson to lead him back to the truck. Wilson insisted he spend twice as long in the disinfectant to make sure his suit was completely scoured.

Back inside Wilson explained the situation to Kimberley. His words were accompanied by the steady drumbeat of the gleba hitting the truck.

"I thought the mutated fungi weren't supposed to be sporing," said Kimberley.

"Perhaps this species is an exception, or maybe they've *all* started sporing. If that's the case we've had it. Let's hope that the gleba catapult mechanism was automatically activated even though the spores hadn't reached maturity."

"But why are those damn things being aimed at the truck?" asked Slocock.

"My guess is that it's the heat from the vehicle that has activated the mechanisms. Heat to the fungus at night probably means rotting organic matter—food—so it lobs its spores in the direction of the heat source."

"You make it sound intelligent," said Slocock with a grimace.

"The conventional *sphaerobolus* species doesn't have an aiming system, does it?" asked Kimberley.

"No," admitted Wilson. "It ejects the gleba in a scattershot pattern. What we've got out there is a definite mutant."

Kimberley winced as another missile slammed into the truck. "And it grew incredibly quickly too. There was no sign of it at dusk."

"So what are we going to do?" asked Slocock.

Wilson realized with a start that Slocock was actually asking *him* for advice. Hiding his satisfaction at this reversal of roles he said, "I suppose we could clear that mess off the windshield and try and drive clear of the fungus, but I doubt we'd get very far before the glass is covered again. So I think we should wait until daylight. My guess is that this heat-activated dispersal mechanism is a purely nocturnal thing."

He was proved right. After spending another two nerve-racking hours listening to the barrage, they were relieved to hear it lessen and then die away.

When it had stopped altogether Wilson and Slocock suited up and went out to clear the windshield and reload the guns. The Stalwart looked as if it had been splattered with red molasses, but no serious damage appeared to have been done.

After a brief meal they got moving again. They crossed the remainder of Fernhill Heath and then turned south onto the M5. The motorway was eerily deserted.

It took them less than half an hour to reach the turn-off, the A4019, that led to Cheltenham and the A40.

As they approached Cheltenham they saw for the first time the effects of the fungus on civilization. Although they were not very far into the infected area, it seemed to Wilson there was a great deal of the fungus about. Many of the houses were covered with the stuff. Grotesque yellow and mauve cascades of froth-like fungus tumbled from windows and hung from roofs like icing on a cake.

There were no people on the streets but occasionally Wilson glimpsed faces at the windows staring at the truck as it roared by. He didn't get a good enough look at them to tell if they were victims of the fungus or not.

Nearer the center of Cheltenham the fungus had a greater hold. It had clearly spread with ease between the closely packed buildings, feeding on all the organic materials available. On some buildings one particular species might be dominant. Brightly colored toadstools would make one office block look like an illustration out of child's book of fairy tales, another would be covered in tiers of horizontal white slabs, but other buildings would have a mixture of growths, like patchwork quilts, as different species fought for control.

They also started seeing people in the streets. Some of them ducked out of sight as the truck approached but others just stood and stared as they drove by. They were all much more drastically affected by the fungus than the victims they'd encountered earlier. Several of them resembled Dr. Carter on the video—they were heavily encrusted with slabs of growth.

Slocock almost lost control of the truck when a man with what appeared to be two heads stepped out in front of them. Wilson saw that the second "head" was a giant puff ball growing from his shoulder. He screamed something at them as they went by, but his words were unintelligible.

There was otherwise little reaction to their passing, though a couple of people—it was impossible to tell if they were male or female—threw bottles at them. Wilson wondered why. Was it due to anti-army feeling or simply because they resented the existence of anyone not infected by the fungus? Probably the latter, he suspected.

Occasionally the road itself was covered with a carpet of fungus. In places it was quite thick and seemed to suck at the tires as the truck passed over it. Wilson guessed that it was feeding on the asphalt.

Then they came to a section of road partially blocked by the ruins of a building that had collapsed into the street. Slocock pulled up and all three of them peered at the fungus-coated wreckage.

"It looks as though the bricks and concrete have been eaten away. What kind of fungus can do that?" asked Kimberley.

"The hyphae of dry-rot fungi—*serpula lacrymans*—can travel through masonry to reach moisture, but they don't actually eat it. This mutated version must do the same at an incredibly fast rate until the brickwork just crumbles away." The pile of rubble across the road presented no serious obstacle to the Stalwart, which was able to climb over it by means of its six large wheels. Then they were on the outskirts of Cheltenham and the road ahead seemed clear.

Wilson yawned, "If no one has any objections I'm going into

the back for some sleep. Unlike you two I didn't get any at all last night."

"We didn't get much either," said Slocock.

"You got a hell of a lot more than me," said Wilson, and grinned at Kimberley.

When he'd crawled through the hatchway and closed it behind him Kimberley said, "I think he knows."

Slocock shrugged. "Who cares? I don't. Do you?"

"It would be less complicated if he didn't know."

He gave her a sidelong glance. "You fancy him at all?"

"No. He's not my type."

Slocock reached across and put his left hand on her crotch. He gripped her hard. She gave a hiss of pain and annoyance and pushed his hand away. "Don't do that!"

Amused, Slocock said, "Oooh, the lady doctor's all uppity today. Doesn't want to remember what she was doing with common old Sergeant Slocock last night."

"That was a one-off event. Don't think for a moment you're going to get second helpings."

Slocock's hand shot out and grabbed her by the hair. She gasped and struggled but he was able to push her head down towards his lap without any trouble. Then he gave her hair a sharp twist. Her scream was muffled.

"You know what to do now, Doctor. And be gentle with it. I feel your teeth in me I'll scalp you."

She unzippered him and freed his already erect penis. As she went to work on him with her tongue he shuddered with pleasure and said hoarsely, "You're a real expert at this, I can tell."

His words were confirmed in the 15 minutes that followed. Several times she brought him to the edge, but just when he felt he was about to explode she seemed to sense it and eased off. Finally she didn't ease off and he came in her mouth with such an intensity of feeling he almost drove off the road.

He let go of her hair. She sat up, unzippered her own pants and kicked herself out of them with an obvious urgency. Then she twisted round, put her left leg across his lap and draped her right foot across the back of his neck.

He glanced at what was being offered. 'No rest for the wicked,' he muttered and put his fingers into its gaping wetness.

Minutes later, as Kimberley, back arched, juddered with a series of uncontrollable spasms, he reflected that the one good thing about the present crisis was the total lack of police cars on the motorway.

After that they rode on in silence for some time. He glanced at her occasionally and was amused to see how quickly she became her usual, cool, poised self. Only the slight flush on her cheeks gave any indication of what had happened.

Finally she said, "I've got to go into the back. I need to use the toilet."

"Try not to wake Buffalo Bill. The less I see of him the better."

Kimberley opened the hatch and murmured, "Oh my God!"

The way she said it made him look around.

On the other side of the hatch there was nothing but a solid wall of yellow fungus.

15

Wilson was still unaware he'd been consumed by the fungus.

He had remained asleep as the growth had filled the rear compartment and he continued to sleep even now.

The growth completely covered him, but as its structure was highly porous, his breathing was unimpeded. He slept on as the fungus ate his clothes and the blanket under him, along with every other organic substance that was accessible to it in the compartment.

When his clothes had been consumed the hyphae proceeded to absorb all his body hair and then entered his various orifices. In his mouth the probing, thread-like hyphae picked his teeth clean of every particle of food; they entered his anus and extended themselves along his rectum, absorbing waste material as they went; in his ears they ate the wax and in his nostrils they consumed the dried mucus.

At the same time the fungus began to dissolve his dead outer-layer of skin. This was what woke him up.

He regained consciousness aware of an intolerable itchiness all over his body.

Then he opened his eyes and saw nothing but total blackness. Then he realized he was covered in something. It was all over him. In his mouth, his nose . . .

He panicked. He kicked and tried to lash out with his arms but it was like trying to swim in syrup. He became frenzied in his efforts to free himself, writhing and twisting against the soft but tenacious substance imprisoning him.

Then suddenly he saw light and heard a voice say incredulously, "Christ, he's still alive!"

Slocock was standing over him, a shovel in his hands. Then Kimberley appeared beside him and helped Wilson pull the strands of yellow fungus from his face and body.

Slocock started to laugh. "Look at him! Like a new-born baby! Bright pink and not a hair on him anywhere!" Wilson was trying to spit something foul out of his mouth. He wanted to throw up. The yellow fungus seemed to be everywhere in the compartment. What had happened? How had it got in?

"The fungus has consumed his entire epidermis, by the look of it," Kimberley told Slocock. "The question is, why didn't it eat the rest of him? It seems to have eaten everything else in here." Then to Wilson she said, "How do you feel? Can you talk?"

"Get me out of this," he gasped.

Together they pulled him free of the mass and the next thing he knew he was sitting on the road and blinking in bright sunlight. He stared down at himself. Slocock was right. His flesh looked very soft and pink, as if it had just been scrubbed very hard, and his pubic hair, and the hair on his legs, was completely gone. He reached up and touched his head. His scalp was smooth. He was totally bald. "Oh Christ," he said.

Slocock was dragging one of the anti-contamination suits out of the yellow chaos that now filled the rear of the truck. He started to put it on.

"Rather late for that, isn't it?" said Kimberley.

"It's to protect me against the solvents I'm going to spray in there," he told her. "We've got to clear that stuff out completely unless you fancy giving it a ride all the way to London."

He unlocked the metal trunk on the back of the truck where the flame-throwers were stored and took out a hand-operated pump. Then he began to spray a white liquid over the fungus. Where the liquid fell the yellow growth began to darken and curl with a sizzling sound.

Kimberley watched for a while, then turned her attention back to Wilson, eyeing him critically. He suddenly became aware of his nakedness, which felt even more acute without any hair, but her interest was obviously a professional one only. She squatted down next to him and gave him a cursory medical examination, feeling his pulse and then peering into his ears and mouth.

"Fascinating," she murmured as she looked into the latter. "Your teeth have probably never been so clean. The fungus has scoured them to the enamel."

"None of it's growing on me anywhere, is it?" he asked anxiously.

"Not that I can see." She examined the rest of him and pronounced him fungus-free. "Hopefully that means the Megacrine is giving us full protection; or maybe you're one of the rare, lucky types who has natural immunity. For my sake I hope it's the former." She looked at her own arms worriedly.

It took Slocock over an hour to clear all the fungus out of the compartment. After that they surveyed the mess that remained. The fungus had stripped the compartment of everything that wasn't made of some inorganic substance. The bunks had been reduced to the metal frames, Slocock's kitbag and the clothes it had contained were gone, and even the labels on the cans of food had vanished.

Slocock picked up a full bottle of whiskey from the debris. It too had lost its label. He wiped the strong-smelling solvent from it and opened it. "Thank God for small mercies," he said and promptly swallowed a quarter of the contents.

Kimberley was salvaging her various medical supplies and instruments from the mess on the floor, her leather medical bag having been consumed too. She held up a small bottle, devoid of a label like all the others, and frowned as she tried to identify the colorless liquid it contained. Then she looked around and sighed.

"To hell with this," she muttered. "All I've got to wear now are these stinking things I've got on. No change of underwear. All the Kleenex has been eaten and . . ." She went over to the small cubicle that housed the chemical toilet . . . it's eaten the toilet paper too. This is getting past a joke."

Slocock burst out laughing. Kimberley looked at him in surprise, then joined in.

Wilson regarded them sourly. When their bout of near-hysteria died down he said, "I'm glad you both find this so amusing. Not only did I almost get killed but now we're *all* exposed to infection. And it's all due to *your* stupid carelessness, Slocock."

Slocock blinked at him, his eyes already bleary from the alcohol. "Huh? Me? What is this shit?"

"You brought the fungus in with you. With one of these." Wilson went over to the gun rack and took down one of the rifles, noticing as he did so that the butt, whatever it was made of, hadn't been eaten away. He displayed the gun to Slocock. "All that crazy beating about in the fungus you were doing last night. A particle of the fungus must have got lodged in the weapon somewhere. In a place where the disinfectant couldn't reach it. So your macho-man, Captain Action act has totally screwed us up."

Slocock's eyes narrowed and his expression grew ugly. "Fuck you, you pathetic-looking piece of crap. You keep your accusations to yourself unless you want me to rip off that little pink imitation of a dick hanging between your legs and stuff it down your throat."

Wilson took a quick step forward and slammed the butt of the rifle into Slocock's face. Slocock grunted and fell backwards. There was a crash as the bottle of whiskey shattered on the floor.

It had been a powerful blow, but Slocock was tough. He came back up from the floor as if on a giant spring, holding the jagged end of the broken whiskey bottle like a dagger.

Then he froze.

Wilson was now pointing the barrel of the rifle at him. "Drop it, Sergeant, or I'll drop you."

Slocock, with blood pouring from his nose and mouth, sneered at him. "You haven't the balls."

"I'll count to five. If you haven't dropped the bottle by then I'll kill you. One . . . two . . . three . . . four . . ." The broken bottle fell from Slocock's hand. "You're a dead man, Wilson."

"Aren't we all?"

Kimberley, who was watching the confrontation with a shocked expression, said, "You're both being ridiculous. We can't afford to fight amongst ourselves."

"We finished fighting. Now we're talking," said Wilson. "Or rather, *I'm* doing the talking, you two will do the listening. From now on I'm in charge. You two will do as I say."

"And if we don't?" sneered Slocock.

Wilson rammed the barrel into the pit of his stomach. Slocock made a sound like a deflating tire and doubled over. "That was my last warning," said Wilson. "Next time I pull the trigger." He turned to Kimberley. "Start hunting through this mess and see if you can find me something to wear, otherwise I'll take lover-boy's clothes, blood and all." Kimberley looked worriedly at Slocock, who was on his knees on the floor clutching at himself. He was struggling to draw in a breath but his diaphragm obviously wasn't working. "I think you've hurt him," she said.

"That was the general idea. You can look after him later. First find me something to wear."

While she searched the lockers and metal trunks Wilson exchanged the rifle for one of the Smith & Wesson .38s. He checked that it was loaded, cocked it and covered Slocock with it.

Kimberley found a pair of oil-stained overalls in the tool box. Wilson climbed into them, keeping the gun on Slocock the whole time. Then he said, "Check that the spare radio is still sealed up."

There was a second VRC353 sealed in a metal container which was to be used if their other radio equipment was rendered useless by the fungus. Kimberley confirmed it was still safe.

"Okay, you can see to him now." He indicated Slocock, who was sitting up now but didn't look capable of any trouble. His face was the color of someone who had recently died, and blood continued to stream from his nose. Kimberley knelt beside him and tried to stanch the flow of blood with his shirt. "I think you've broken his nose," she told Wilson.

"It looked broken before."

He waited impatiently until the bleeding had stopped and

Slocock had recovered to the point of being able to get to his feet again. The fight appeared to have gone out of his eyes but Wilson wasn't taking that for granted. He knew Slocock was an old hand at fighting hard and dirty, and he didn't intend letting his guard down.

"Okay, Sergeant, you think you can drive now?"

Slocock was still holding his lower stomach. "It feels like my guts are ruptured."

Wilson fired the revolver. Kimberley screamed as the bullet, which narrowly missed the side of Slocock's head, ricochetted off the forward hatch and zinged past her.

"Jesus! You're going to kill us all!" shouted Slocock fearfully, his eyes wide with shock.

Wilson nodded and said calmly, "I'm not very good with guns. Haven't touched one since my ROTC days at college." He cocked the revolver again and pointed it at Slocock's forehead. "You think you can drive now?"

"Yeah."

"Then let's get going." He turned to Kimberley. "You're going to stay back here. Be an uncomfortable ride, I know, but I can't afford to have you up front. You might get in the way if there's any trouble with your friend. Basically I just can't trust you not to side with him." He glanced at the gun rack and came to a decision. With the exception of one of the Sterling L2A3 submachine guns he threw the contents of the rack out through the open, and now useless, airlock.

"That's crazy! We're going to need those!" cried Slocock.

"Get up front and start the engine," ordered Wilson. He picked up the remaining Sterling and hung it over his shoulder, then followed Slocock towards the hatchway. On the way he noticed something on the floor. He bent down and scooped it up. Then he tossed it over to Kimberley. "I don't think you'll have a need for this again this trip."

She stared speechlessly at the half-empty jar of vaseline.

In the driver's cab Wilson sat as far away as possible from Slocock, jamming the Sterling between himself and the door. The revolver he kept in his hand.

Slocock was revving up the powerful eight cylinder Rolls-Royce engine prior to moving off. Wilson had a thought. He told him to cut it.

"Well, make up your bloody mind," he growled as he obeyed. "Now what?"

"Get Buxton on the radio. I want to talk to him."

When Slocock had made contact with the Wolverhampton base it took a couple of minutes before Buxton could be located and summoned to the radio. While he waited Wilson thought he could hear shooting in the background.

When Buxton did come on the channel his voice sounded high-pitched and ragged. "Wilson? That you? Why on earth haven't you kept in contact? What are conditions like in London? Have you located your wife yet?"

"I'm afraid we're still west of Oxford," said Wilson, wondering what was wrong with Buxton. "Had a few problems that delayed us. Also we've lost our sterile environment. But we're okay and pushing on now. We'll be in London by late afternoon for sure."

Buxton just said, "Oh Christ." The shooting in the background was getting louder.

"What's happening where you are? What's all that gunfire?"

"We've been cut off. The infected area outflanked us before we could pull out. And now some of my men have mutinied. They want to join forces with the other rebel units and make a push to the coast. They'll probably succeed, too. The rebels are well armed and numerous. They've got several Chieftain and Challenger tanks. But if they reach the coast in any number, the French are almost certain to execute their plan to drop nuclear bombs on the country ahead of schedule."

"Look, we still have a chance of achieving our mission," Wilson told him. "Our vehicle is still mobile and we're still all healthy. Even though we're exposed now, the Megacrine is obviously giving us adequate protection against infection."

There was silence at the other end. Then Buxton said, "We got a message from Bangor. The surviving two volunteers on Megacrine have both succumbed to fungal infection since you left."

Unexpectedly, Kimberley took the news worst of all.

When Wilson told her over the intercom what Buxton had said she cried, "Oh Christ, it's all over then! We're finished! We have no protection at all! We're going to end up looking like those people in the street. We've got to turn back!"

"Take it easy. The drug must be giving us *some* protection, even if it's only for a limited period. We may still have enough time to get to London and find Jane."

"To *hell* with London and Jane! Let's go back! Now, before that horrible stuff starts growing on us!"

"Kimberley, I suggest you take a long drink from one of the Sergeant's remaining bottles of scotch and calm down. You're getting hysterical. If it makes you feel better, get into one of the suits."

"What good would that do? It's too *late*! We're . . ."

Wilson switched off the intercom. "She's starting to crack up."

"But she's right," said Slocock. "I agree with her. We turn back. Those rebel army units will punch a hole through the barriers all the way to the coast. We could follow in their tracks."

Wilson waved the .38 at him. "You don't have a vote in this anymore, Sergeant, and neither does she. Get moving or I'll put a bullet in your brain and drive this thing to London myself. You showed me how, remember?"

Slocock restarted the engine.

PART THREE

I

They did a wide detour to the south of Oxford, almost as far south as Abingdon, and then sped across country until they encountered the M40 north of High Wycombe. They had only made one stop along the way. They'd both grown used to seeing the increasingly bizarre growths as they penetrated deeper into the infected area—such as the red candyfloss-like fungus that hung from the branches of most of the trees, and the colonies of huge mushrooms and toadstools, some of which were over 20 feet tall—but as they were driving across a field Slocock suddenly swore and braked the truck.

"What the hell is *that*?" he asked, pointing to a growth a few yards away. It looked like the erect penis of a sleeping giant. It was about six feet high and its head or cap was covered with a thick black slime. Several birds were stuck fast in the stuff, their feathers plastered to their bodies. A few of them were still struggling, but the rest were still.

"Looks like an oversized version of *phallus impudicus*," said Wilson, "Also known more commonly as the stinkhorn. Usually they only grow up to between six and nine inches in length."

Slocock stared at the thing. "I need a drink. I feel sick. Go fetch me a bottle of scotch, would you? I promise you no tricks."

"Sure. As soon as I happen to look the other way I get the bottle on my head." He gestured with the .38. "Get going."

When they reached the M40 Wilson decided to check on Kimberley. He switched on the intercom and asked her if she was okay. Her reply alarmed him.

"Get back here right away, please, Barry!" she cried, sounding on the edge of panic. "Quickly!"

Deciding it would be safe to leave Slocock alone, as there was nothing he could use as a weapon in the cab, Wilson opened the hatch and crawled through.

He was startled to see her standing there naked, a small mirror in her hand. She looked distressed.

"Barry, you've got to help me! I've tried to look everywhere but I'm sure there are places I can't see, even with the mirror." She turned her back to him. "Is there any of it growing there? Please check carefully . . ."

He'd realized by then what she was talking about. He was shocked at the state she was in. He'd pegged her as someone who would never lose their self-control and it was disturbing to see her going to pieces like this.

He examined her back and pronounced her clear of any fungal growth.

She bent over, practically shoving her bottom in his face. "What about down there?" She parted her buttocks. He looked, reflecting that in other circumstances his feelings about what she was doing would be very different. Instead her panic was beginning to infect him too. He became aware of several itchy patches on his body. He told her he couldn't see any fungus on her.

She still wasn't satisfied and made him examine the back of her neck and head.

"Look," he said as he probed through her hair, "this is all a waste of time. If we find any sign of infection on us it's already too late. Why not just calm down? There's nothing you can do."

She spun round, eyes flashing angrily. "I'm *not* going to let myself turn into one of those *things*. Look at me! I'm beautiful, aren't I? Do you think I could stand to have that horrible stuff growing on me? Spreading *through* me?"

"But how can you stop it?"

She indicated a nearby can of powerful solvent. "I'd burn it off. And if that didn't work I'd kill myself. At least I'd die clean."

He knew she meant what she said. Brutally he said, "You should have thought of all this before you volunteered to come here."

"But I was sure the Megacrine would protect us! I can't understand why it failed."

In an attempt to calm her down he said, not really believing it himself, "Perhaps that other stuff you've been pumping into us is the important factor. The . . ." He couldn't remember the drug's name.

"Inosine pranobex?" She shook her head. "The two human guinea pigs back at Bangor were on that too, but it didn't help them."

"But they were already dying. They both had cancer. Their immune systems were no longer functioning properly. But we three are all healthy. The drug may be giving us an edge those two poor bastards didn't have."

He was satisfied to see a faint touch of hope appear in her eyes. "I suppose that is possible," she said slowly. "Their T-lymphocyte cells, even with their number increased, would have been concentrated around the tumors. They wouldn't have been able to cope with an invasion of fungal cells as well."

"Right," he said with more confidence then he felt. "Now calm down and get dressed." He found one of Slocock's bottles and opened it. He took several long swallows and then offered the whiskey to her. "Drink some of this. Doctor's orders."

She even managed a brief flicker of a smile as she took the bottle.

When he left, she was getting dressed. She seemed to have recovered most of her composure, but he suspected the crisis had only temporarily been averted.

Back in the driver's cab he handed Slocock the cup of whiskey he'd decided to bring back with him. Might as well try to keep everyone happy.

Slocock took it without thanks and drained it in one gulp. He expelled a satisfied burp and said, "So what's the trouble back there?"

"Nothing. She was having a panic attack for no reason." *Yet*, he added to himself.

"You reassured her, eh?"

"Yeah, sort of." He scratched at an itchy patch on his chest.

"You give her a quick poke as well?"

"What?" He looked at Slocock in surprise. "No, of course I didn't."

"You should have. You're the one with the power now. She'll be ripe for you. Just come on a bit strong with her. She likes that. But I guess you know that already. I figure you were eavesdropping last night on the intercom."

"As my old friend Flannery once said, 'Life is nothing but a giant cess-pool, which is why it's advisable to swim with your mouth shut'."

He opened the front of his overalls and examined the itchy patch on his chest. The skin still looked bright pink but there was no sign of anything else. He wondered how'd he'd react when he *did* find something.

As they came nearer to London the fungus got worse. The built-up areas they were passing through were totally unrecognizable beneath their surreal fungal coverings and it was only when they saw a barely visible sign for Denham that they knew where they were.

Houses were soft mounds, all traces of man-made sharpness gone. Between the buildings grew the giant mushrooms and toadstools, and occasionally giant white puff-balls the size of radar domes. The fungi were clearly the victors in this brief war between them and mankind. Very soon there would be no trace left of humanity's handiwork. Or of man himself.

But for the moment the former dominant species was still in evidence. Wilson kept glimpsing people in the street or standing in fungus-draped doorways. Not that they still looked like people. Every one he saw had been blighted by the fungus in some way. If there was a small percentage of people who possessed some miraculous immunity to infection, he saw no sign of them. If they existed at all, perhaps they were in hiding.

Past Denham they began to encounter difficulties on the highway. A continuous thick carpet of hyphae grew on all the road surfaces. This presented no real problem to the Stalwart's tires; however in places great ropy strands stretched across the road like jungle suspension bridges.

Most of the time the truck was capable of breaking through them, but eventually they came to a section where the strands grew so thickly, the vehicle was forced to come to a halt.

"We're stuck!" exclaimed Wilson, staring around. "It's like being in the middle of a giant spider's web!"

"We could burn our way through the rest of the stuff. There's not much more ahead," said Slocock. "But . . ." He didn't go on.

"But what?"

"But you'll have to do it. I don't like . . ." He swallowed and went on. "I don't like handling flame-throwers. But I'll show you how to operate the damn thing."

Wilson hesitated. Was this a trick? A scheme to get the upper hand somehow? He *sounded* genuine, though. He seemed actually embarrassed at having to admit this weakness.

Wilson decided to give him the benefit of the doubt. "Okay. Let's get outside."

On the way through the rear compartment Wilson explained the reason for the stop to Kimberley. She insisted on putting on one of the anti-contamination suits before they opened the back doors. He was impatient at the delay, knowing that the suit's protection was probably only an illusory one now, but thought it best to humor her.

When they stepped outside they entered a bizarre, fairyland world of bright colors and soft, furry surfaces. Even speech sounded alien in this strange new environment with the omnipresent fungus absorbing all vibrations. The result was an awful, muffled stillness in the air.

Wilson stood unsteadily on the springy substance covering the road while Slocock extracted one of the flame-throwers from its locker. Not only was he keeping a suspicious eye on Slocock, he was also trying to watch the numerous figures he glimpsed lurking in the buildings on either side of the street.

Slocock handed him the flame-thrower and from then on all his attention had to be on it while Slocock explained how it worked. Slocock showed him how to light the burner and then how to operate the valve that would send the gas-ejected fuel spurting out some 15 to 20 feet. "Remember, short bursts only," warned Slocock, his distaste for the weapon all too evident on his face.

As Wilson struggled into the harness Slocock dryly offered to hold the Sterling for him. Wilson just smiled without saying anything. He stuck the .38 in the front pocket of the overalls where it was within easy reach and took hold of the business end of the flame-thrower, which needed both hands.

Slocock had backed the truck several yards from the fungus strands that had blocked them, giving Wilson plenty of room to use the flame-thrower. As he unleashed the terrible stream of liquid fire with its deafening roar he quite understood Slocock's phobic dislike of the weapon. It was indeed an infernal device.

The fungus offered no resistance to the fire. The thick strands blackened, bubbled, then melted away, leaving only an awful stink in the air. Wilson had soon burned his way through most of them.

A warning shout from Slocock between bursts made him look round. He saw four misshapen figures rushing toward them. All were carrying clubs. One had an axe. Behind them, further back, a larger group was massing on the side of the road.

He acted without thinking. He spun round and sprayed the four nearest figures with the liquid fire.

One of them went down as if hit by a high-pressure hose. He, or she, went rolling across the fungus-covered road scattering burning fragments like a Catherine wheel. The other three, who hadn't taken the full brunt of the jet of fire, staggered about flailing their arms as their fungal crusts burned fiercely. They made hideous, high-pitched wailing sounds that cut like a knife into Wilson.

Shocked at what he'd done, he stood there staring at them helplessly, the lowered snout of the flame-thrower still dribbling fire onto the fungus matting. He was only dimly aware of the bigger group fleeing in all directions.

"Quickly, damn it!" he heard Slocock shout. "Before they make another try."

He snapped back into life and followed Slocock to the rear of the Stalwart. Slocock switched the weapon off, then helped Wilson out of its harness. They flung it into the locker and then hurried inside, slamming the door. Kimberley, still encased in her suit, made urgent gestures at them as they pushed by her towards the front cab but Wilson was in no mood to explain the situation to her.

When he reached the cab he saw that two of his victims were, horrifyingly, still writhing as they burned. The other two were unmoving, blackened shapes.

While Slocock started the engine Wilson pulled down the mini-gun control and starting firing blindly. Eventually he managed to hit his targets. They shuddered and stopped moving.

"Don't waste any more bullets," cautioned Slocock as he sent the truck surging forward. The Stalwart cut through the remaining strands of the fungus and sped down the road.

"Why did they attack us?" cried Wilson, the image of the four fungus-covered figures enveloped in flames still searing his retinas. "I didn't mean to do that to them."

"A good thing you did. Otherwise, we'd be dead by now."

"But *why* did they attack? We weren't threatening them at all."

"But we were threatening their beloved fungus. Killing it."

"Their *beloved* fungus. What do you mean?"

"Who knows what those poor bastards think anymore in all that stuff? I reckon it's a case of 'if you can't beat it, join it.' The ones the fungus doesn't kill probably feel grateful to it, despite being turned into walking mushrooms."

Their progress towards the center of London got slower and slower. Often the roads were blocked completely and they had to make numerous detours until they could find an alternate route. On one occasion, as they were traveling through what they guessed to be Wembley, they were stopped dead by a huge toadstool that completely filled the road. Its trunk—it was too big to be called a stem—was at least 15 feet in diameter and its cap dwarfed the houses on either side of the street.

Then later, as they were crawling along the Harrow Road past Kensal Green, they were attacked by another mob—a big one numbering several hundred. They emerged from the surrounding, suffocating dreamscape like creatures from the worst nightmare imaginable. Large creatures, slow and bulbous, with stubby appendages, bearing iron bars, bricks and bottles. They formed a solid line across the road in front of the truck. Slocock didn't slow down.

Missiles began to hit the windshield, some bouncing off, some shattering.

The Stalwart plowed into the mass of obscenely soft bodies. Wilson's stomach turned over as he heard the *thud*, *thud* of the impacts and felt the big wheels going over things . . .

There were muffled cries. A spurt of greenish liquid suddenly obscured part of the windshield.

Wilson threw up.

Then the truck started to slow down, its wheels spinning as it fought a losing struggle with the mass of bodies around and in front of it.

"Shoot, for Christ's sake, shoot!" yelled Slocock as he fought to push the truck onward.

Wilson hesitated for only a few moments. He told himself the creatures out there were no longer people. The fungus had turned them into something else.

He opened fire with the minigun and then the big machine gun. The things that were still capable of movement began, at last, to scatter.

The engine strained as the truck attempted to climb the soft, slippery mound in front of it.

A lurch as the cab tilted back . . . and then they were over it and free.

Slocock sent the truck hurtling down the Harrow Road, smashing through anything that got in his way, no matter what it or who it was.

They were just passing what Wilson barely recognized as the turning into Ladbroke Grove when in front of them stepped yet another missile-wielding creature. But this one was holding a bottle with a rag stuffed into the top. And the rag was burning.

The creature flung the gasoline bomb too soon. Instead of hitting the truck, it shattered on the road ahead of them. But at the sight of the spreading pool of fire Slocock screamed and tugged violently on the wheel.

The Stalwart went into an uncontrollable skid. It shot across the road and straight into the corner of a fungus-covered building.

Wilson felt himself flung forward into the windshield, and then there was nothing but blackness.

2

Chaos. Pain. Confusion.

Wilson was battered by all three as he floated up from unconsciousness. His head throbbed and there was a taste of blood in his mouth. What had happened? And what was making that terrible noise?

He opened his eyes, trying to orientate himself. It took him several seconds to realize that the Stalwart was now lying on its side. It had tipped over onto the passenger side and he was wedged up against the door.

There was no sign of Slocock. The emergency hatch was still sealed, so that meant he must have gone through to the rear compartment.

Clang. The cab vibrated from yet another violent impact. It sounded as if someone was using a sledge-hammer. He could also hear hoarse cries and yells. Lots of them.

He couldn't see anything through the windshield—it had frosted over from the crash—and all he could see through the window on the driver's side, now above him, was the evening sky.

Wilson struggled to extricate himself from his awkward position. At the same time he groped for the Sterling submachine gun. He couldn't find it. It was gone. So was the .38.

Something filled the window above him. He looked up and saw a head that resembled a Halloween pumpkin. It hissed at him. At that moment the windshield caved inward and Wilson was showered with powdered glass. He shut his eyes and raised an arm to protect himself.

He felt a rush of warm, moist air and then there were hands pulling at his body. Hands that seemed to be encased in thick, soft mittens.

He tried to fend them off, his flesh crawling at their touch and at the thought of the infection they carried, but there were too many of them. Despite his struggles he was inexorably dragged out of the cab through the shattered windshield. *Like a turtle being ripped out of its shell*, he thought. *I'm totally defenseless now. They've got me.*

They were everywhere he looked. Caricatures of human beings. The pure stuff of nightmare. Some were doubled over from the weight of fungal growth they carried on their bodies, some were thin and partially eaten away, covered in only a sheen of mold. And others were so deformed by the fungus it was hard to believe they were of human origin at all.

Making nerve-jangling cries they hustled him over the rubble to the rear of the truck. He glimpsed a white suit in the midst of another throng of the creatures ahead, then saw the familiar short black hair and pale face. He shouted Kimberley's name and heard her cry his in return. But then she was swallowed up in the mass of obscenely soft, fungus-coated bodies.

At least she was still alive, he thought as he was half-shoved, half-carried along the Harrow Road, back along the way they'd come, but what had happened to Slocock?

Slocock fought to control his panic. His biggest fear was that the truck would be hit by another petrol bomb. He wanted to get out through the emergency hatch and get as far away from this death trap as he could, but his soldier's conditioning warned him to resist the urge. It would be, he knew, suicide to venture out there unarmed.

So he forced himself to take a deep breath, and then began to hunt around under Wilson's crumpled body for the Sterling. As he did this, to his surprise, Wilson groaned. He'd presumed he was dead. Well, thought Slocock, he soon would be, and good riddance. He located the Sterling and also the revolver. For a moment he was tempted to put a bullet through Wilson's head, but decided not to bother. Why waste ammunition?

Ammunition. Again he stopped himself from using the emergency hatch. Instead he maneuvered open, with difficulty, the hatch leading into the back of the truck and crawled through.

The rear compartment was a shambles. Kimberley, still in her anti-contamination suit, was moving feebly under an oxygen cylinder that had come loose from its wall bracket.

He pulled the cylinder off her, then ignored her as he set about collecting several full clips of 9mm ammunition for the Sterling. He shoved them into his belt and was about to open the rear door when he thought of something else.

His prayers were answered. One bottle of whiskey had survived the crash. He picked it up and smiled at it as if greeting his dearest friend.

By then Kimberley had taken her helmet off and was struggling to stand up. "What happened?" she gasped.

"Bit of an accident. Drove into the side of a house," he said as he got the door to the airlock open. "Better get moving if you're coming with me."

Kimberley gave a groan of pain as her left leg buckled beneath her and she fell. "My leg!" she cried. "You're going to have to help me!"

"Sorry. It's every man for himself. Beside, you'd only slow me down." He hauled himself up into the airlock, which now lay horizontal at chest height, taking care not to break the bottle of whiskey.

"You can't just leave me!"

"Watch me." He pushed the outer door open, slid through the airlock, then jumped down to the ground. He almost slipped on the fungal matting but managed to keep his balance. It was fortunate that he did. Three lumbering figures were coming straight toward him, clubs in their hands. They were less than five yards away.

Operating the Sterling with just one hand—he was holding the scotch in the other—he sprayed them with bullets. All three of them dropped but in the grey twilight he could see more of them coming down the Harrow Road towards the crashed Stalwart.

He hurried across the intersection and into Ladbroke Grove. It was difficult running on the slippery, yielding surface but by adopting a kind of sliding shuffle he found he could keep up a fair pace.

He crossed over the bridge that spanned the Grand Union Canal. The canal itself couldn't be seen. It was concealed beneath a thick profusion of different fungi, some of them quite huge. The plentiful supply of water had obviously allowed the fungi to grow even larger than usual along the canal's route. The giant, brightly colored toadstools marched in both directions in straight columns as if someone had deliberately arranged them in formation.

Slocock hurried on and then took cover beside a fungus draped building that he felt instinctively had once been a pub. He set his bottle down carefully between his feet and waited. He didn't have to wait long.

They came hurrying along the road, using the same sort of shuffle he had. There were only about a dozen of them. He guessed the rest of the mob he'd seen were concentrating on the truck. He felt a momentary pang of regret at having had to leave Kimberley behind, but quickly suppressed it.

When the shuffling group had passed his hiding place he stepped out and opened fire. He got most of them with the long burst but two were still standing when he'd emptied the clip.

Unhurriedly he pulled the empty clip out, threw it away and replaced it with a fresh one. The two creatures hesitated, then started toward him. He felt strangely calm and detached as they approached. Even when one of them spoke, unexpectedly, in a clear, educated *woman's* voice he experienced no real surprise. He was beyond surprise.

"Don't shoot," she said. "We just want to talk to you."

He let them get closer. One of them was holding a crowbar. When they were about six feet away and he could plainly see the loathsome details of the crusts that covered them he opened fire.

As the bullets smashed into them they were both sent sprawling backward, but the one with the crow-bar flung it at Slocock as he, or she, fell. He dodged to one side and the bar missed him. But then it bounced off the fibrous wall behind and landed right on the whiskey bottle.

Slocock stared down in distress at the shattered remains. He felt like crying.

He walked over to the two fallen fungus victims and kicked the nearest one in the side. His boot penetrated the crust and body beneath it by several inches, making a dry *snap* sound. When he pulled the boot free he saw a greenish liquid begin to trickle out of the cavity he'd made.

Incuriously he examined the other corpse. This one was lying in a pool of ordinary red blood. He wondered if this was the woman. He also wondered, if he ripped off all the fungal crusts, whether he'd find the body of a perfectly ordinary woman underneath.

He doubted it, but the idea made him think of his wife Marge. They'd had some good times together, at first. But then he'd realized their sexual needs were out of sync. He'd never thought of himself as undersexed, but she had made him feel that way after a while. She wanted it every night, no matter what. And when he couldn't manage it every night, or at least without being able to conceal the effort it took, she began to nag and taunt him about it, which only made the situation worse. And after that things just went to pieces.

Where was she now? he wondered idly. He knew she'd moved to London after leaving Aldershot, but she'd never sent him her new address. Was she still alive, and if so, did she look like one of these things lying on the ground in front of him?

His thoughts turned to Kimberley and their love-making of the night before. Again he felt regret at having to leave her behind and briefly considered returning to the truck, but he dismissed it as a suicidal idea. There had been too many of the things coming down the road and, hell, it was probably too late now.

But the thought that he might never see again a plague-free, naked woman in whatever time he had left depressed him profoundly. "Christ, I need a drink," he muttered and stared wistfully at the broken bottle.

Then he walked back to the building and peered in through the strands of fungus that clung to the window. It *was* a pub, he realized.

He picked up the crowbar and started to prise the door open. The wood, riddled with fungus, disintegrated immediately and he was able to step into the gloomy interior. The stink in there was bad and he held his nose while he waited for his eyes to adjust to the darkness.

Despite the spongy growths that looked like giant green egg yolks covering the walls, ceiling and floor, Slocock saw that he was in a bar. A shapeless mound by one wall had to be the bar itself.

He made his way to it, stepping warily around the circular growths on the floor. He was about to step behind the bar when a hand grabbed his ankle.

He glanced down and saw what appeared to be an emaciated human arm protruding from an oblong mound of fungus on the floor. He pulled his leg free and stepped back, the Sterling ready to fire.

A reedy, whispery voice said to him, "Help me . . . please help me."

Slocock began to make out what the shape on the floor was. It was a man, or rather the remains of a man. His body seemed to be part of the fungus growing out of the floor, though apart from his head, his torso, and one arm there wasn't much left of him.

"Help me," the thing whispered.

"Sure thing," said Slocock with a smile and pulled the trigger. "Closing time, pal."

He then went behind the bar and began wiping aside the moss-like growths covering the bottles and glasses. The labels had been eaten away but he was soon able to identify a full bottle of scotch. He opened it and took a long drink. "Canadian Club," he told himself happily.

He went to the front of the bar and perched himself on top of a fungus-draped bar stool. Its upholstery was gone but its tubular steel frame was still solid. The fungus squelched under his buttocks.

He placed the Sterling on the pulpy surface of the bar and then laid out the spare clips of ammunition beside it. There were four of them left. Thirty-two rounds in each. One hundred and twenty-eight bullets, plus what was left in the clip on the gun. Oh, and the four bullets left in the .38. He smiled and took another long drink from the bottle. He'd be able to kill a hell of a lot of things with all that, provided he used the ammunition sparingly.

It was going to be a good night.

Wilson had given up trying to resist. Now he just let himself be carried away by the tide of shoving and pulling creatures. He was dimly aware that he and Kimberley—he got brief glimpses of her up ahead—had been dragged back up along the Harrow Road to the spot where they'd first encountered the big mob.

And now he was being hustled through some gateway and down a lane. In the fading light he saw that they were inside a large, sprawling cemetery, the tombstones still visible among the fungi. He was mildly surprised; he'd driven along the Harrow Road many times but had never really noticed the existence of this large place before.

The horde of creatures surrounding them seemed to be increasing in size as they were carried along a lane bounded on both sides by a profusion of fungal growths amid tall obelisks and blockhouse-like mausoleums. Wilson guessed that the cemetery was a more than ideal source of nourishment for the fungi.

The lane widened and Wilson saw that they were approaching a strange building that seemed to be a Victorian reproduction of a Greek or Roman temple. In spite of the fungus growing on it he could see the rows of columns extending out on either side from a tall central structure, forming a square with one side open.

Dominating this curious scene was the biggest fungus Wilson had ever seen. It grew in the center of the square beside the main building which it easily dwarfed. It was either a mushroom or a toadstool and it stood at least 40 to 50 feet high.

He saw several of the fungus victims fall on their knees as they approached it and he realized, with a shock, that they were praying to it.

Then the mob formed a circle in front of the giant fungus, or rather *beneath* it as its huge cap was about 100 feet in diameter.

Wilson saw Kimberley thrust into the center of the circle. She staggered a few feet and fell. She was obviously having trouble walking. He struggled against the ones who held him, but couldn't break free. He was forced to watch helplessly as several of the creatures converged on Kimberley.

They pulled the contamination suit off her, then stripped her of her clothes. After that they pinned her on her back on the ground, her body spread-eagled.

What were they going to do to her, he wondered frantically. Rape her?

No; he soon saw that the violation of her body they intended was not a sexual one.

One of the creatures came forward carrying an armful of colored fungus. He kneeled beside Kimberley and began to rub chunks of the material over her body.

Kimberley screamed and struggled but soon her body was soaked with juices from the fungus.

And then they forced pieces of the stuff down her throat.

After that they backed away from her, watching her as she writhed on the ground, choking and retching.

Wilson was suddenly propelled forward into the circle.

It was his turn now.

3

Wilson's arms ached. He'd been tied to one of the columns for several hours, his arms pulled back behind him and secured by thick strands of woven fungus.

The night was pitch-black apart from the faint illumination provided by the moon. He could just make out the pale shape of Kimberley's body similarly tied a few columns away. He had tried speaking to her, but she wouldn't answer. She seemed to be well and truly sunk in her personal pit of despair.

He shifted his position in yet another vain attempt to ease the strain on his arms. And he was also dying for a drink of water. It was a hot night and the air was thick with humidity and the fecal odor of the fungus.

He stank of it himself. His whole body was smeared with it, it was in his hair, and he could still taste it from the time they had forced him to eat the stuff and swallow its juices.

After the "ceremony" he and Kimberley had been tied naked to the columns, and their captors had settled down to wait. Wilson had quickly realized what they were waiting for, and so had Kimberley, to judge by her frightened sobbing.

Every so often one of the creatures would come and examine them, looking for signs that the fungus was growing on them. So far the examinations had proved negative, to his intense relief, but he knew it could only be a matter of time before one of them, or both, displayed the inevitable stigmata. What would happen then he had no idea. Presumably they'd be released to be full-fledged members of this fungus-loving crowd.

What a total fiasco, he told himself bitterly. Instead of even beginning to search for Jane and her papers he'd ended up in this situation. No transportation, no weapons, not even any clothes . . . and certainly not even the remotest hope of achieving what he'd come here to do. He had begun to realize that the whole mission had been a wild long-shot from the very start.

He heard a sound, turned and saw a shadowy outline shuffling towards him. Most of their captors seemed to be sleeping now but one or two had obviously stayed awake to carry out the inspections.

Then, as the bulbous figure drew nearer, Wilson saw the moonlight being reflected off something in his hand. Something metallic.

He had a knife.

What was this? Had they got tired of waiting? Or was this some kind of ritual sacrifice? Wilson tried to edge his way around the column, but he was bound too tightly.

He tensed himself as the creature halted beside him, waiting for the awful pain of the knife blow.

"Dr. Wilson, I presume?" wheezed a soft voice.

Wilson was so startled he was unable to reply.

"Dr. Wilson?" repeated the voice. "Dr. Barry Wilson?"

"Yes," he said, his voice cracking. "Who are you?"

"A great fan of your Flannery books, Dr. Wilson. I thought your last one, *The Meaning of Liffey*, was marvelous."

"Uh, thanks." Wilson couldn't believe he was having this conversation. Was it some fungus-induced hallucination?

The creature made an odd, rustling sound that Wilson realized he'd heard before. Then, "Sorry, Dr. Wilson. Couldn't resist my little joke. I still have a sense of humor if not much else. My name is Dr. Bruce Carter. I've been waiting for you." He began slicing through the strands with his knife.

Wilson remembered the Public Health investigator on the video. He felt a surge of renewed hope as he was cut free. "God!" he cried. "How on earth did you find us?"

"Shush, not so loud or you'll wake our friends. I'll explain everything later. First let's get your companion free."

Kimberley raised her head as they approached her and said in a dull, apathetic voice, "What are you doing?"

"Escaping," said Wilson, and told her who Carter was.

Her reaction was to mutter, "What's the use? We might as well stay here. We're finished. I can feel it growing on me."

As Carter cut her free of the bindings Wilson quickly ran his hands over her face, torso and limbs. Her skin felt smooth to his touch. "You're fine," he told her. "Come on, get up. We're getting out of here."

He pulled her to her feet. She leaned against him and groaned. "My leg. I hurt my knee when the truck crashed. I don't think I can walk."

"You'd better," he said roughly. "I certainly can't carry you."

With Carter in the lead, and Kimberley hobbling painfully, they picked their way quietly through the mass of sleeping creatures. Even though Wilson knew they were human beings under their fungal shells he was unable to regard them as people any longer. And he was thankful the darkness prevented him from getting a good look at Carter.

They made it to the lane that led through the cemetery to the entrance. As they hurried along it as fast as they could, which wasn't very fast due to Kimberley's leg and the fact that Carter couldn't manage much more than a shuffle, Wilson began to relax a little. He again asked Carter how he'd found them.

"Knew you . . . were coming," he wheezed with difficulty. "Intercepted radio messages meant for you. Posted lookouts on the main western approaches still open into London . . . there are still a few of us who can call our brains our own, though for how much longer I don't know. My own thoughts are getting stranger all the time . . . a sign the fungus is affecting my mind."

He paused to suck in air, making a sound like water going down a drain.

He continued, "The physiological changes the fungi are imposing on their unwilling hosts are quite interesting from the scientific point of view. The effects are many and varied, but there does seem to be a major trend toward the mutating fungi somehow harnessing human intelligence for their own survival purposes.

"But I'm digressing—another indication of mental deterioration, I fear—I was telling you how I came to be here. The lookout I'd posted south of here heard all the shooting and guessed it might be you. He fired a flare to alert me and I came as fast as I could, which wasn't very fast, I'm afraid. I found your abandoned vehicle and knew it *was* you."

"But how did you know we'd be in that weird temple place back there?"

"That's where they take all their victims. They hunt for people who don't show any signs of infection. There are a few such around—natural immunity, I gather—but they are very rare. If they still don't get infected in spite of everything our friends at the temple do to them, they are then killed as heretics. Like one of those old witchcraft trials—you can't win either way."

Kimberley gave a piercing shriek. Wilson turned and got a fleeting impression of something rushing at them out of the darkness. He pushed Kimberley to one side and struck blindly at the shape.

He felt his fist make contact with something brittle. There was a sound like a stalk of celery being snapped in two. At the same moment something hard caught him a glancing blow on his left shoulder.

Dazed, he swung his fist again but met nothing but empty air. Then he discovered that his attacker was stretched out on the ground in front of him.

Wilson knelt down and gingerly examined the thing with his fingertips. He said wonderingly, "Damn, its neck's broken. I didn't hit it *that* hard."

"Many of them are so riddled with the fungus, their bodies are becoming extremely fragile," said Carter. "They are probably more fungus than human now. I suspect the same thing is happening to me . . . uh oh, *listen*!"

In the distance, from the direction they'd come, there was a murmur of voices—a kind of angry buzzing as if a bee hive was slowly coming to life.

"I'm afraid the lady's cry carried too far," wheezed Carter. "They'll be coming after us."

Wilson stood up. He was now holding the iron bar that the creature had attacked him with. He took Kimberley by the arm.

They weren't far from the entrance. As they emerged into Harrow Road Wilson hesitated. "How far are we from the truck?" he asked Carter urgently. "I was confused on the way here."

"About half a mile."

The murmur of angry voices was getting closer now.

"We'll have to try and make it. Come on, as fast as you can!"

It was downhill, but as the three of them slipped and staggered along the fungus-covered roadway Wilson realized their pursuers would catch them before they reached the truck.

He voiced his fear to Carter, who was wheezing painfully as he shuffled along. His reply was hard to hear. "Might . . . be . . . able . . . to slow . . . them down," he gasped. "Noticed . . . some bird's nest fungi . . . on the way here."

About 50 yards further on he veered toward the high wall that bounded the cemetery. As Wilson followed him he saw a large number of white, trumpet-shaped growths protruding from the wall.

"Giant *cyathus*," said Wilson as they hurried past the growths. He glanced over his shoulder. The first few pursuers were closing in, though the bulk of the mob was still a fair way back. Wilson guessed that the ones leading the pack were less fungus-riddled than the others and had more control of their limbs.

As they passed the end of the long row of *cyathus* fungi Carter said, "Strike the wall as hard as you can. With the bar."

Wilson suddenly saw what he had in mind. He stopped and swung the bar at the wall. The impact jarred his arms. He swung again.

Something like a cricket ball with a spring attached flew out of one of the nearest trumpet-shaped fungus and shot clear across the road.

He hit the wall several more times and was gratified to see a full-scale eruption of the things all along the row of fungi. One of their pursuers screamed. Wilson could imagine what was happening to him.

In conventional *cyathus* fungi there are a dozen or so little round objects called peridioles containing the badio-spores. The peridioles rest on spring-like hyphal coils. When the fungus is mature the impact of raindrops falling onto it is enough to activate the mechanism. The peridioles fly out of the trumpet and the trailing spring-like hyphae sticks to any leaf or twig it touches, coiling itself tightly.

With fungi this size the hyphae must be capable of exerting a tremendous amount of pressure.

And judging by the increasing number of screams in the darkness they were doing just that.

"Good idea," cried Wilson as he caught up with Carter's shambling form. He was about to clap him on the shoulder but held back his hand at the last moment, remembering what Carter's shoulder consisted of.

"A delaying tactic only," wheezed Carter. "Killed a few, no doubt, but it won't stop the others for long. What do you have in mind when we reach the truck?"

"It all depends on what's still there." He didn't continue.

Finally the bulk of the Stalwart, lying on its side amid the rubble of the partially demolished building, appeared out of the gloom. Wilson rushed forward and anxiously examined the locker containing the flame-throwers. It was still intact. There were signs that someone had tried to batter it open but had failed.

Wilson prayed he would be more successful. He could hear the mob approaching down the road.

In a frenzy he attacked the lock with the iron bar. He rained blows on it, ignoring the jarring pain of each impact. Something gave. He was able to wrench the door open.

Hurriedly he dragged out one of the weapons, trying to remember Slocock's instructions for operating it.

"Oh God," cried Kimberley in a small, terrified voice. A tall shape covered with what appeared to be tennis balls lurched out of the darkness. Wilson, still struggling to light the thing, thrust the end of the flame-thrower into the creature's face. There was a crunch and it fell, mewling, to the ground. But there were several others close behind.

At last! He had found the switch that ignited the after-burner. And now all he had to do was turn a valve—there was a satisfying hiss of pressure—and . . .

The flame shot out with its terrible, ear-splitting roar, a great, dribbling tongue of fire that was so bright, after all the hours of being in near total darkness, it hurt Wilson's eyes to look at it.

Its glare illuminated a scene out of a painting by Hieronymous Bosch. The road, already transformed by the fungus into a surreal landscape, was filled with a mass of creatures that could have only come straight from hell.

It even occurred to Wilson, as he stood there pouring fire into the midst of the screaming horde, that he was actually *in* hell. That he had perhaps died of a heart attack in his Irish cottage and all that had happened in the past few days had been his personal descent into eternal torment . . .

He cut the flow of fire, remembering Slocock's instructions to use short bursts only.

Several of the creatures were burning. They ran about in circles, screeching and waving their arms as their fungus-riddled bodies sizzled and crackled. Wilson looked at them without emotion. He was numb.

He unleashed the fire again.

The crowd broke up, the creatures running in all directions. Some ran with flames streaming in the night air behind them . . .

He moved forward, letting loose another burst of fire—aiming the nozzle high as he would a garden hose and scribing a wide arc of burning liquid in front of him. Then he shut it off and surveyed his handiwork. There were numerous fires all around, and the air stank.

Apart from the things that lay still or feebly kicking in the flames there was no sign of the fungus creatures. The area was deserted.

He turned and headed back to the truck. Kimberley and Carter stood motionless beside it, vaguely illuminated by the flickering red glow from the various fires.

Wilson realized that Carter was indistinguishable from the creatures he'd just burned, and Kimberley scarcely appeared human either. Her hair matted to her skull, her body stained with fungi juices and tarnished red by the glow, she looked like a female demon.

He wondered what he looked like, naked and carrying a flame-thrower.

Something gave a low, wailing cry as it burned.

He didn't look round. He suddenly felt very tired.

"What now?" he asked Carter helplessly.

"We go to see your wife," said Carter.

"My wife?" repeated Wilson, astonished. "You know where Jane is?"

"I've known for several days now."

"She's still alive! Thank God for that!" cried Wilson. "But what about my kids? My son and daughter? Are they with her?"

"I'm sorry," wheezed Carter. "I don't know. I haven't actually *seen* your wife. I know where she's located but I can't get to her. Her followers guard her too well."

"What? Her *followers*? What are you talking about?"

"Your wife's a very important woman now, Dr. Wilson," said Carter, and made the dry, rustling sound which was his equivalent of laughter. "In fact you could say she's gone up in the world. In more ways than one."

4

Slocock was drunk. He'd finished the entire bottle of whiskey and was now opening a second one. A lesser man, he knew, would be unconscious on the floor by now and probably inhaling vomit, but he had the constitution of a Chieftain tank.

"There's no two ways 'bout it," he announced to the empty, fungus-ridden bar as he lurched around with the fresh bottle. "I can hold my fucking liquor." He stopped as something crunched under his boot. Swaying, he peered down and saw he'd stepped on the remains of the fungus victim he'd shot earlier. His boot had crushed its fragile skull.

"Oh, 'scuse me, fella," he said to it and weaved his way back to the bar stool. He climbed carefully onto it and took another long drink. Then he picked up the Sterling and fired a long burst in the air, raking the ceiling with bullets. Chunks of fungus and plaster fell everywhere.

"Time, gentlemen! Time!" he yelled. "Can I have your glasses *please*." He started to laugh then stopped when he felt a stab of pain in his forehead. A hangover already? But he hadn't finished drinking yet. He ran his head over his sweaty forehead. Then, surprised, he ran it over again. He couldn't believe it. Hair! His receding hairline was growing back! Thick and luxuriant!

He grinned happily to himself. "This calls for another drink," he told the empty bar as he raised the bottle. He was too drunk to wonder why his hair had started to grow back, he just took it for granted as some kind of strange miracle. After all, these were strange times . . .

He remembered how, when he was younger with a full head of hair, he'd never had any trouble picking up women. Now that he had all his hair back, he was confident it would be as easy for him again.

He placed the bottle lovingly down his shirt front, gathered up the ammunition clips, and slid off the stool. His mind was made up. He would go and find a woman. One that wasn't covered in all that muck. There had to be at least one or two around.

He staggered out of the ruined pub and began to make his way down Ladbroke Grove. He felt very happy. He had three important things—a bottle of whiskey, a gun, and a hard-on. What more could a man want, apart from a woman?

As he progressed, unsteadily, down the street he became aware of others using the thoroughfare. They shuffled and scuttled furtively in the shadows as if they didn't want to be seen, and who could blame them, thought Slocock. On one occasion he glimpsed a creature that appeared to be covered with fluid-bloated condoms. As drunk as he was, the sight nauseated him, and he immediately shot the creature with the .38.

He also shot four people—things—who were joined together by thick strands of fungus like a Siamese quartet. "Doing you a favor," he told them as he opened fire while they tried to flee from him in four directions at once.

He lost track of the time as he wandered about on his quest for a woman. He also became confused as to where he was. Under their blankets of fungus all the streets looked the same.

Then, when he was getting low on both whiskey and ammunition—he'd shot a lot of creatures by that time—he saw what he'd been searching for. A woman. An untouched woman. A woman with clean, white skin. And she was all his.

All he had to do was get rid of the two fungus-ridden maggots who were in the process of raping her.

At least the truck's lights were still working. Wilson blinked in the sudden brightness, then helped Carter clamber down into the wrecked rear compartment, forcing himself to overcome his aversion to touching the man. It was the first time he'd had a chance really to see Carter, and it took an effort to keep telling himself that there was a human being underneath all those huge, wart-like crusts.

Carter read his mind. Peering at him with his one visible eye he wheezed, "Not a pretty sight, eh? Think a hair-piece would help? A big one, maybe?" He made his odd laughing sound again.

Wilson, feeling embarrassed, looked away. Kimberley, he saw, was splashing herself with a trickle from the drinking water tank in an attempt to wash off the dried fungal juices. At the same time she was anxiously examining her body for signs of infection. He automatically glanced down at his own body, half-expecting to see the fungus somewhere on him. But as far as he could tell, through all the soot and fungus stains, he was still infection-free.

Observing this, Carter commented, "It's remarkable you two have both escaped the fungus so far, even though you've been exposed for a considerable time."

Wilson told him about the drugs they'd been using.

"But not any longer," said Kimberley bitterly, gesturing at the smashed glass littering the overturned compartment. Their captors had done a thorough job of breaking everything that was breakable.

An unpleasant thought suddenly occurred to Wilson. He immediately checked the locker containing the spare radio, and saw at once the seals were broken. One look inside was enough to show him that the set was beyond repair.

"Well, that's it then," he said sourly. "Even if we get Jane to talk there's no way we can transmit the information."

"Yes, there is," said Carter. "I'm a one-time radio ham. Cost my father a fortune when I was a teenager, and I had to give it up when I began my medical studies, but there still isn't much I don't know about radios. I've been cannibalizing equipment at British Telecom, building makeshift receivers. The fungus gets into them pretty quickly but I've been able to keep a step ahead of it. That's how I picked up those messages meant for you. I'm sure I can rig up a transmitter. There are still plenty of spare parts sealed up at the Post Office Tower."

"And you say that's where Jane is? At the Tower?"

Carter nodded his bulbous head. "Right at the very top. Her followers guard the only way up there."

Wilson frowned. He was still having trouble accepting the incredible story that Carter had told him about Jane. "You say these people actually *worship* her? But why?"

"They obviously believe her when she tells them she created the fungus and controls it. Her followers are all women, by the way, though what the significance is of that I don't know yet."

"But what's she *doing* in the top of Post Office Tower?" asked Wilson.

"I've heard rumors she's established some sort of laboratory up there."

"You think she might be working on a way of stopping the fungus?"

"From what I hear about her I doubt it very much."

Wilson sighed. "Well, at least she's still alive and rational enough to organize a lab. That means she's probably still capable of looking after the kids. I'm sure she wouldn't let any harm come to them, no matter what the state of her mind." He turned to Kimberley. "Stop wasting that water." She was still splashing it over herself and frantically peering at her skin.

"I have to know if it's on me yet," she cried, then, as before, turned her back to him. "Can you see it anywhere? Tell me the truth."

He gave her back a cursory look. "You're fine," he told her, then salvaged a cup from the debris. "Move aside, I'm thirsty."

"You don't seem to care!" she accused him as he gulped down a cupful of water. "We're going to look like that *thing* over there, and you don't give a damn!"

She was pointing at Carter.

Wilson said nothing. Instead he filled the cup again and handed it to Carter.

Kimberley muttered something under her breath and went to the rear door. "Where are you going?" Wilson asked her.

"I'm going outside for a pee. I can hardly have one in here."

That was true. The cubicle housing the chemical toilet was now horizontal. "Don't go too far from the truck," he warned her. "And keep an eye out for anything moving."

He watched her as she climbed out of the open airlock. She seemed completely oblivious to her nakedness and he felt a sluggish revival of his desire for her—a desire that had been dormant for some time.

"A very attractive woman," commented Carter.

"Yes," agreed Wilson, uncomfortably aware that his partial arousal was physically evident. "I wish she had something to wear. I wish *I* had something to wear."

Carter made his wheezing laugh and said, "You don't have any spare clothing with you?"

Wilson told him about the fungus attack that had cleaned them out of everything organic.

"Well," said Carter, "You really don't need clothes in London anymore, as far as the climate is concerned. The fungus seems to have raised the average temperature by at least five degrees. And the humidity has increased, too."

"And after a while the fungus even clothes you as well," said Wilson bitterly.

"Yes, there is that," conceded Carter. "But you two have been lucky so far. Perhaps those drugs have given you permanent immunity."

"Perhaps," said Wilson though he didn't believe it for a second.

After a pause, Carter said, "An odd choice for this expedition. Your traveling companion, I mean."

"Kimberley? At first I didn't think so. Seemed as hard as nails. But then when she found out the Megacrine drug wasn't all it was cracked up to be she began to go to pieces. I guess she believed she was 100 percent safe from the fungus, otherwise she would never have come."

"And why exactly has she come?"

"That, Dr. Carter, is a good question."

Kimberley moved some distance away from the truck, taking care to avoid the still-smoldering remains of the creatures. The knot of terror in the pit of her stomach was like an unbearable physical pain. She felt so scared and helpless, but there was nowhere she could run, nowhere she could hide to avoid the inevitable infection. It was probably growing inside her already . . .

At the beginning the odds for pulling off her gamble had seemed in her favor, but now . . .

She squatted down amid the rubble of the building. At least her knee was feeling better. Something rustled behind her. She was just turning her head to see when a hand was clamped over her mouth and she was pulled roughly backward.

She tried to scream but couldn't make a sound. Then the hand withdrew. She opened her mouth to draw breath but as she did so something rubbery was thrust into it, gagging her. She recognized the foul taste of fungus.

The next thing she knew she was being pulled along by her feet like a human sled. She tried to resist, digging her fingers into the ground, but it was useless. The fungal matting covering the road was too smooth.

As she was pulled quickly along, her head was gently buffeted by undulations and small growths in the carpet of fungus. Soon she was feeling quite dazed.

It was some time before she was able to get a clear look at what had captured her. Eventually she was able to keep her head raised long enough to see. There were two of them—one holding each leg—both very thin and emaciated. In the dim moonlight she saw ulcerous craters all over their backs.

She had no idea how far they'd traveled from the truck when the creatures finally stopped and let go of her legs. The continual buffeting had left her semi-conscious and at first she was only half aware that she was hearing voices.

"Go on . . . you first."

"No, no . . . I'll wait . . . all that running . . . have to catch my breath."

They sounded like two people suffering from very bad laryngitis. She wondered what they were talking about.

"You're scared you can't *do* it any more."

"I *can*. I just need a bit of time. Go on. You warm her up for me. I can see you're ready from here . . . it's enormous."

Christ, she thought, *they're going to rape me. I've come all this way to be gang-banged by two pathetic, dying zombies.*

She tried to sit up but as she did so she was punched in the face. She fell back onto the fungus, bright lights flashing in her eyes . . .

Then her legs were being roughly parted. A heavy body, hot and sticky, was suddenly on top of her and at the same time she felt something being brutally thrust into her. It was unnaturally large and it hurt like hell.

Her horror and disgust gave her extra strength. She violently wrenched her body to one side, simultaneously giving the rapist a powerful shove with her arms . . .

There was a distinct *crunch*. Then a thin, wailing scream. She looked up and saw him kneeling there clutching at his crotch. Blood spurted out between his fingers.

His companion cried, "What's wrong? What did she do to you?"

The other one just continued to scream. It was then that Kimberley became aware that he was *still* inside her. She realized that his grotesque member was so diseased with fungus it had simply snapped off.

Her revulsion sent a hot stream of vomit rushing up her throat. She was noisily sick, getting rid of the chunks of her fungus gag. Then she reached between her legs, trying to extract . . .

A hand grabbed her hair, jerked her head around. She found herself staring into what was once a face. She'd seen such faces before. In Africa. On untreated leprosy victims.

"I'm gonna kill you for what you done to me!" the face screeched.

Then, somewhere nearby, there was a sound like an animal burping very loudly and the top half of the face ceased to exist. The thing slumped toward her, spattering her with its blood. She screamed and shoved it away from her.

Its companion obviously didn't know what was going on. It

was looking around wildly in all directions. The hidden animal made a much longer sound this time and the creature's body jerked and shuddered as if it were trying to shake itself to pieces. Then it fell.

Silence.

A figure stepped into view out of the shadows of a building. And then she heard a familiar voice say, in a drunken slur, "It's the British Army to the rescue, Doc. And not bad shooting if I do say so myself."

It was Slocock. The feeling of relief was so acute, she almost passed out. "Thank God," she gasped.

He came closer, and she was able to see his face.

She started to scream.

5

Slocock couldn't understand what was wrong with Kimberley. Here he'd just saved her from those two stinking pox-bags and she was acting like he was Count Dracula out for a bite.

"Here, Kim, it's me! Good ol' Sergeant Slocock. The man with the magic fingers." He bent over her, brushing the thick hair out of his eyes (it was amazing how quickly it had grown). But she just screamed again and pushed herself away from him, scuttling backwards on her hands and heels like a giant crab.

The hair! That's why she didn't recognize him. It probably made him look 10 years younger, at least.

He started after her, saying, "Kim, you silly bitch, it's me. I've just got more hair, that's all."

She sprang to her feet, turned and ran—slipping and sliding over the fungus. He cursed to himself and started to follow her. No telling what other trouble the silly slut would get herself into if he didn't catch up with her.

He yelled her name again but she put on speed and disappeared around a corner. He hurried after her—and ran straight into the gateway of hell.

All he saw was a brilliant red flash that rushed straight at him and consumed him. The next moment the fluid of his eyeballs had solidified like the boiled white of an egg. He felt his flesh crackling and shriveling, but so far his shocked nervous system hadn't been able to register any pain. For a few terrible seconds Slocock was aware of what was happening to him and then, mercifully, the intense heat detonated the 9mm ammunition in the remaining clip stuck in his belt. One of the bullets penetrated his brain . . .

Wilson switched off the flame-thrower and warily approached the smoldering, blackened shape. He'd been surprised when he'd heard the ammunition going up. He hadn't noticed that the creature was armed.

He sighed and he stared at the charred form. He didn't like the way he was finding it easier to use this horrible weapon on the creatures. A bad sign . . .

He looked around for Kimberley. At first he couldn't see her, but then spotted her squatting on the ground some distance away. "Kimberley, you okay?" he called as he approached her.

"Stay away from me!" she cried. "Don't come near me!"

He stopped, frowning, then turned to Carter, who was following him, and shrugged.

Kimberley succeeded in extracting the fungus-phallus from herself. With a shudder of disgust she flung it as far away as she could, then threw up again. But this time there was nothing but bile. After dry retching for a time she managed to get to her feet and stagger towards Wilson and Carter.

"Are you all right?" Wilson asked her.

"I'm never ever going to be all right again," she said. She remembered Slocock's face—or what was left of it. The thick tendrils growing out of his skull like worms . . .

She had seen her own future in his face.

"Do you know who you just incinerated over there?" she asked Wilson, pointing at the smoking body.

"What do you mean? How could I know?"

She shook her head. "It doesn't matter. Not now."

Carter shuffled up to them. "We really should get moving, if the lady is up to it. We have a long way to go."

"Can you walk, Kimberley?" asked Wilson. "Or do you want to rest awhile?"

"I'm fine," she said listlessly.

"I suggest we head on down toward the Bayswater Road," said Carter. "The Paddington route is impassable. The Westway and Marylebone overpass have collapsed. One of the mutated fungi seems to be causing a chemical change in all concrete structures as a byproduct of its metabolism. In a few months I doubt there'll be a building standing in all of London."

They set off in their shuffling, shambling gait, Wilson straining under the weight of the flame-thrower. Behind them, already forgotten—even by Kimberley—Slocock's burned remains began to cool.

By the time they reached the Bayswater Road it was beginning to get light—Wilson guessed it must be 5 a.m. at least—and the world of the fungus was revealed in all its horrible glory.

Hyde Park was an impenetrable forest of giant growths, some of the huge toadstools or mushrooms being almost as large as the one they'd seen in the cemetery. Many of them were brightly colored, and the overall effect was like that of a scene from some old Disney cartoon.

On the other side of the street the buildings were concealed under vast, moldering heaps of fungal growth. Only the tallest buildings revealed their man-made origins as the fungus thinned out near the top and sections of glass, brickwork, or metal showed through.

They encountered a fair number of creatures—*people,* Wilson had to remind himself—along the way, and on two occasions he was forced to demonstrate the power of the flame-thrower in order to disperse gathering mobs. The trouble was that his and Kimberley's clearly untouched bodies attracted attention. His big fear was that the weapon would run out of fuel before they reached the Post Office Tower.

Wilson noticed that Kimberley's continual inspection of her body was becoming even more obsessive. And her concern was catching—he found himself looking down at himself every minute or so and running tentative fingers across his face and back.

"You're still fine as far as I can see," Carter told him as he checked himself for the hundredth time.

Wilson glanced at him with embarrassment. "Sorry, can't help it. It's the waiting. I'll probably feel relieved when I actually see something on me."

"I doubt it," said Carter.

"You've coped. You're handling the whole thing very well."

"No choice."

Wilson lowered his voice. "There's always death. I'm afraid that's going to be her reaction when it finally hits her." He indicated Kimberley, who was walking a little ahead of them. "Did you consider killing yourself when it happened to you?"

"It crossed my mind," admitted Carter. "But I'm not a brave man. Death still scares me. I want to live as long as I can, even like this."

They were passing through Marble Arch now. The arch itself was invisible under the fungus. Ahead stretched Oxford Street—a bizarre fungal canyon.

Wilson suggested taking a short cut through the back streets but Carter advised against it, explaining that many of the smaller streets were completely blocked. "Best if we head along Oxford Street and then go up Tottenham Court Road," he said.

A few minutes later Wilson stopped and stared hard at the Babylonian Gardens of hanging fungal rot and yeasty strands that obscured the front of what was obviously a large building. He experienced a shock of recognition. "Good Lord, that must be Selfridges! I've got to take a quick look, do you mind?"

Carter said hesitantly, "I don't think we have the time—"

But Wilson was already pushing his way through the fibrous curtain and Carter, and Kimberley, had no choice but to follow him.

They entered Selfridges' department store through a shattered window. Inside, the store was not filled with the homogeneous mass of fungus that Wilson expected but instead contained a mad variety of different growths everywhere, and on everything, in bright, mottled profusion. The atmosphere was heavy with damp and barely breathable with its moldering stench.

Wilson stared around in disbelief. "We used to shop in here—Jane and I—a lot. In the early days, when we were still . . ." His voice dried up. For some reason the ruined interior of the famous department store was having a greater impact on him than anything else he'd seen so far. He suddenly realized how much the fungus had destroyed. Even if it was finally overcome things would never be the same again. London definitely wouldn't, and nor would he.

"Come on, let's get going," he said roughly.

They moved on along Oxford Street. At the end stood the Centrepoint high-rise, its highest three or four floors entirely clear of the fungus. It gave the impression of something bursting free of its shroud, but Wilson guessed that the fungus would continue to grow inexorably upward until it covered even this tall building's roof.

They turned into Tottenham Court Road. As they did so there was a loud rumble from the direction of the City. Wilson asked Carter what it was.

"Building collapsing," said Carter. "It's happening all the time, but getting more frequent as the fungi eat through the concrete."

Wilson looked back at Centrepoint and wondered what kind of crash it would make when it finally toppled over.

They approached the Post Office Tower. It resembled an enormous mushroom. Fungus, dark and malevolent, had accumulated around its bulbous summit.

Somewhere up there was Jane and, hopefully, his two children. But what did they look like now? Like one of the horrors he could see across the road, calmly munching on a piece of fungus?

The sight sickened him, yet at the same time made him aware of how hungry he was. A thought occurred to him.

"What do you do for food?" he asked Carter.

"I do the same as that poor unfortunate," said Carter, gesturing at the creature opposite, who resembled an overripe Michelin Man. "I eat the fungus. Some of it actually tastes quite good. But then, I always liked mushrooms." He made his wheezing laughing sound.

The fungus made the tower seem even bigger than it was, and as they approached it the tall structure loomed over them oppressively.

Wilson remembered the one occasion he'd gone to the top of it. It had been years ago, back in the days when there was a revolving restaurant and observatory open to the public. Before the IRA had blown out a chunk of the place with a bomb in '73 . . .

They drew closer to the base of the tower. "Where's your radio equipment located?" Wilson asked Carter.

"In the adjacent Telecom building, not in the tower itself. But there is probably stuff I could use up in the TV control room if I could get access to it. And I'm going to need to rig my antenna as high as possible. I can't transmit from the first floor. The fungus appears to absorb radio waves."

"Where will you get your power from?"

"There's a diesel generator in the basement. It's kept running by your wife's people."

Wilson was surprised. "Why?"

"She needs the power for whatever she's doing up there."

Carter led them to a doorway partially obscured by fungus. They entered a dank, foul-smelling stairwell. Wilson checked the flame-thrower. There was a reassuring slosh of fuel in its tank. He ignited the after-burner. "You show me the way up to the top," he told Carter, "then wait until I come back. If I don't come back you'll know I've failed." He turned to Kimberley. "Same goes for you."

She shook her head. "I'm coming up with you. I haven't come all this distance to stop now."

"Look, you'll be in my way if I have to use this thing."

"I'll stay well behind you," she said firmly. "But I *am* coming with you."

He sighed. He wasn't going to waste time or energy arguing with her.

Carter led them to the first floor of the Telecom building and then along a passageway to the base of the tower. "It's a long climb," he warned. "The basement generator isn't enough to power the elevators."

"Do you know where these guards of Jane's are located?"

"Anywhere between here and the top. And I don't know exactly how many there are of them, either. They patrol in groups of two or three. Carry things like steel spikes as weapons. Vicious bitches, too. I've seen them in action, so don't let the fact they're all women inhibit you with that weapon."

"It hasn't yet," said Wilson grimly, thinking that many of the creatures he'd torched so far had probably been female under their fungal crusts.

Carter pushed aside a curtain of hyphae to reveal the entrance to the spiral staircase leading to the top of the tower. The walls and stairs themselves were covered with damp-looking fungus. It looked like the cancerous orifice of some giant animal.

Wilson wanted to turn and run. Sweat began to pour out of him. He didn't want to know what was awaiting him at the top of the stairs.

"What's the matter?" asked Kimberley impatiently.

"Nothing." He stepped forward.

6

Climbing the staircase was difficult. The layer of smooth fungus made everything slippery, and Wilson kept losing his footing. Nor did the weight of the flame-thrower help matters.

The only source of illumination was from the weapon's after-burner, but Wilson was beginning to think that its red glow was more of a handicap than an advantage. It meant that whoever was guarding the staircase could see them coming, and he was sure it wasn't his imagination that he could hear faint sounds up ahead. As if someone were backing away from him as he climbed . . .

He halted to rest his aching legs. And as he did so an idea occurred to him.

He heard Kimberley laboring up the stairs behind him. "Stay where you are," he called softly to her. "I'm coming back down. There's something back there I want to check out."

"What are you talking about?" she called back irritably. "I can't see anything to check."

"Shush," he warned, turning so that the nozzle of the weapon pointed down the stairs and its glow was shielded by his body. Straining his ears he was positive he heard a movement above. He also felt a slight stirring of air against his bare skin. Someone was creeping down the staircase toward him.

He moved as close to the outer wall as he could, then quickly turned and aimed the nozzle upward.

He let loose a long gush of fire that splashed off the opposite wall above and disappeared round the curve of the central pillar of the spiral. Over the roar of the flamethrower, which was deafening in the enclosed space, he was satisfied to hear a high-pitched scream.

Then he screamed himself as some of the liquid fire dribbled back down the stairs and brushed his left foot when he didn't move out of the way fast enough.

At the same time a figure appeared around the curve of the stairs. It was burning fiercely and as it staggered blindly downward it kept slamming itself against the wall, trying to put out the flames.

"Watch out, Kimberley!" he cried as it stumbled past him, searing his skin with its heat.

The thing disappeared around the curve and then he heard Kimberley scream. There was a sound of something falling down the stairs and more screaming.

"Kim, are you okay?"

He was relieved to hear her say, shakily, "I think so. She grabbed my arm but then she tripped and fell. I've got a couple of burns but I don't think they're serious. Why the hell didn't you *warn* me you were going to do that?"

"I would have warned it—her—at the same time. And whoever else is up ahead."

He continued onward. The glow from the weapon revealed another burned body further up the stairs. This one, fortunately, was not moving.

While he was staring at the corpse there was a metallic *clang* and a metal rod with a sharpened end narrowly missed his head after ricochetting off the wall. He reacted quickly, sending a quick burst of flame upwards. There was a cry of pain and the sound of receding footsteps.

Wilson picked up speed. *Keep them on the run*, he told himself. *Don't give them a chance to plan something clever.*

Nothing else happened for about five minutes, then he heard a series of loud crashes up ahead. He couldn't understand their significance at first, then realized what was happening. A large metal object was rolling down the stairs.

He pressed himself against the central pillar and yelled to Kimberley to do the same. The noise was getting louder. It sounded huge, whatever it was, and moving fast. No chance of outrunning it.

It was right above him now—only yards away. He tensed himself.

Suddenly a large cylinder—like a big water heater—came hurtling round the curve. Wilson felt an agonizing stab of pain in his left thigh, and then the thing clattered past him.

"Kim . . . ?" he called when the tank had rolled past her position.

"I'm still here. It missed me."

"You were lucky." He felt his thigh. There was a large flap of skin hanging loose and a lot of blood. But he knew he'd got off lightly. His main hope was that they couldn't find something even bigger to roll down. If the tank had been only a couple of feet wider it would have swept them both down the staircase. All the way to the bottom.

Gritting his teeth against the pain in his leg he started upward again. Then stopped almost immediately. He could hear footsteps padding down from above. They were coming to see the effects of their weapon.

He waited until they were just around the bend, then turned on the flame-thrower, shutting his ears to the female screams that resulted. A burning figure stumbled around the curve as before and seemed to reach its arms out to him before collapsing. Again fire dribbled down the stairs, making the fungus sizzle and producing a stench.

He moved on. He passed three more bodies at different intervals, all of them smoldering. The one that had got the furthest up the stairs was twitching feebly. He ignored it and kept going.

The climb went on for ages. He felt certain he was almost at the top but every time he rounded the curve there was just another expanse of stairway ahead.

It was during one of his increasingly frequent halts to catch his breath that he heard a woman's voice call out clearly from the darkness ahead, "Turn back. You can't get past us, even with your devil's man weapon. There are too many of us. We are blocking the way completely."

With a shock he realized he recognized the voice.

"Hilary!" he gasped. "Is that you?" The last time he'd seen Hilary Burne-Smith was at a pub in Highgate, the night he'd told her that he thought their brief affair should come to an end. It was during one of those periods when he was making a periodic attempt to repair his relationship with Jane, shortly before he gave up and left for Ireland.

Hilary Burne-Smith had been the newest of Jane's assistants, fresh from Cambridge and a stranger to London. Feeling sorry for her, they'd invited her to dinner on several occasions. He'd given her a ride home each time, and then one night she'd invited him up to her place for coffee, and . . .

He knew he hadn't taken advantage of a lonely, homesick young woman who could have been rather attractive if she'd lost a bit of weight; he was aware that she'd done the seducing, not him. But he certainly hadn't resisted one iota. And sex with her turned out to be surprisingly good. Hilary in bed was a different Hilary from the somewhat shy and very correct young lady he'd come to know across the dinner table. He would have been quite happy to continue the affair except for the nagging guilt, and there was more guilt when he told her it was over, because her reaction had been unexpectedly emotional. There had been lots of tears and he'd sat there, all eyes on him, feeling like a heel.

That had been over two years ago. He hadn't seen her since. And now here she was confronting him in the dark in this hell-hole.

"You?" she said with surprise. "It can't be!"

"I'm afraid it is. Barry Wilson in the flesh. How are you, Hilary?"

There was a long pause before she answered. "Why are you here? Why have you murdered my sisters?"

Wilson flinched at the word "murdered." "I have to see Jane . . . speak to her. It's very important. She's the only hope of saving the rest of mankind from the fungus."

In the darkness Hilary laughed. To Wilson it seemed, under the circumstances, a shocking sound.

Then she said, "*Man*kind is finished. A new order has arisen to cleanse the world of his unholy deeds. The great softness will spread across the globe and blur the edges of Man's harsh works before consuming them totally. And Man himself will also be consumed. Only those who welcome the softness—who become part of it—will be saved." She spoke the words as if reciting a litany.

Wearily he said, "The only softness around here is in your brain. *Christ*, Hilary, only a short time ago you were a scientist! You can't have changed so completely, so quickly. There must still be a glimmer of rationality in you somewhere. So *listen* to me, Hilary. Pay attention to what I'm saying! You're sick! But you can still help protect others who aren't sick!"

There was another long pause and when she spoke again her voice sounded different. "You're right, Barry . . . I am . . . *am* sick. What am I going to do? Can you help me? I can't seem . . . to think . . . straight anymore . . ." Her voice broke and he realized she was crying. Then he heard her coming down the stairs toward him. She stepped hesitantly into the red glow coming from the after-burner. She was still recognizably a woman. Her fungus consisted of a thin mosslike mold that looked like some kind of skin-tight costume covering every inch of her. Her full, heavy breasts swayed as she came slowly down the stairs. Her eyes—those very familiar eyes—were stricken with despair.

"Hilary . . ." he whispered, a terrible sadness welling up through him. She held out her arms to him.

"Help me," she pleaded.

Then she lunged.

Before he knew what was happening he was losing his balance and she had almost wrested the flame-thrower nozzle out of his grip. Then he was on his back, the tanks digging painfully into his flesh, and she was on top of him, snarling as she pulled the nozzle out of his reach with one hand and squeezed his wind-pipe with the other.

Suddenly, to his amazement, a metal tongue suddenly grew out of her chest, right between her breasts. She stiffened and screamed. It was then that he saw Kimberley behind her, one of their metal spears in her hands.

"Hurry," she said as she shoved Hilary to one side, "I can hear her friends coming."

She helped him up. He fumbled with the nozzle. The footsteps sounded very close.

They came round the curve like a solid wall. There must have been a dozen of them at least. At the same moment, he ignited the flame-thrower.

The next minute or so was literally something out of hell.

At the end of it he stood there, choking on fumes, while around him bodies writhed and moaned. He somehow found Kimberley through all the smoke and together they hurried on upward, anxious to get away from that hideous scene.

They encountered no more of the "sisters" and finally reached the top of the stairway. They emerged into the lowest level of the observatory. The fungus was everywhere, covering even the windows. A quick search revealed that the area was empty.

So were the next few levels. But when they entered the section that had once housed the rotating restaurant, they found themselves blinking in a blaze of bright light.

Warily they stepped into the circular room, waiting for their eyes to adjust to the unexpected brightness.

The second thing that surprised him was the total absence of fungus in the place. It was draped over the exteriors of the windows but there was none inside at all. The floor, ceiling, and various pieces of laboratory equipment scattered around were all pristine clean.

Then a voice said, from so close behind him he jumped, "Why on earth did you shave off all your hair, Barry? Being bald doesn't suit you at all."

It was Jane.

7

He turned, dreading what he was going to see.

But what he did see was totally unexpected.

Jane stood there exactly as he remembered her. She seemed completely untouched by the fungus. She was wearing a white lab coat, but her legs and feet were bare and there was not a single blemish on them. Her face and hands were unmarked too; in fact she appeared to be positively glowing with good health.

She advanced toward them with a welcoming smile and Wilson experienced a wave of unreality. It was as if he and Kimberley had dropped in to pay a social call, except that they were both naked, covered in soot and blood, and he was carrying a flame-thrower.

Jane stopped some feet away and ran a critical eye over both of them. She frowned slightly, then smiled again. "Who's your friend, Barry?" she asked, gesturing at Kimberley. "She looks quite attractive under all that muck."

Before he could answer Kimberley said, "My name is Kimberley Fairchild. We've met before, at the London University Conference two years ago."

"Really?" There was no sign of recognition in her eyes as she again examined Kimberley's body. Wilson realized she was looking for a sign of the fungus. She was obviously puzzled that there was none on either of them.

"Jane, where are Simon and Jessica?" he asked urgently. "Are they all right?"

"What? Oh, yes, they're fine," she said dismissively.

"Where are they? I want to see them."

She ignored him. She was now sweeping her gaze up and down his body again. "How very strange that neither of you show any sign of the fungus. The odds against both of you having natural immunity must be very high. I don't understand it."

"We were taking drugs to protect ourselves. They seemed to have worked, so far," he said. "Look, about the children—"

"Drugs? What drugs?" Jane's eyes glittered brightly. It was the first firm indication of her state of mind. His hopes that the children might be safe after all began to plummet. He told her quickly about the Megacrine and the other drugs.

She smiled with what appeared to be relief. "Short term protection, possibly, but nothing more. You've both been lucky."

"So have you. Unless you're concealing it."

"No. I am untouched too." She opened the lab coat. She wore nothing underneath it. The rest of her body glowed with the same unnatural good health as her face. "I have been spared by the Earth Mother in order to finish my work. When it is complete I will gladly submit to her embrace."

Wilson glanced at Kimberley, trying to give her a silent warning to let him do all the talking. Then, to Jane, he said, "Earth Mother?"

Jane gestured at the fungus clinging to the outside of the windows. "There is her blessed manifestation. All around you. We are in her womb."

"Jane," he said gently, "that stuff is poison. It's killing people right across the country. It has to be stopped."

She gave him a pitying look. "For a time, I didn't understand, either. When it began I thought I'd done something terrible. But then the Earth Mother showed me the truth: that I was the instrument chosen by her to transform the world into her image. To bring about the end of man's evil domination of the planet and allow the Earth Mother to regain what is rightfully hers."

"Jane, the fungus is causing suffering wherever it spreads."

"There is always pain at the time of birth. But once man has been cleansed from the world the Earth Mother will protect and sustain her children. We will become one with nature instead of fighting against her. There will be no more hunger or pain. We will be enfolded and nourished by her forever."

"I see," he said softly. It was hopeless. Unable to cope with the enormity of what she had unleashed, her mind had become completely unhinged. She had convinced herself that she had somehow achieved her original objective—that her fungus would end world hunger.

"And what is this work you mentioned that you had to finish?" he asked.

"I must find a way of overcoming the inhibiting factor that is preventing the fungi from sporing, and I must also alter the fungi so that the few unfortunate people who resist infection will be able to succumb to the Earth Mother's embrace."

He nodded, maintaining his outward calm while his blood turned to ice water. "And have you had any success yet?"

"I am close to solving the sporing problem, I feel sure of it." She indicated a row of incubators that followed the curve of the outer wall. "And when I have succeeded I will take the new spores to the roof and release them into the air. They will also include the new genetic factor to enable the fungi to embrace the few who are naturally immune. *That* problem I have already solved, though I need to conduct further tests to be certain. But with the help of you two, the whole process will be speeded up."

"Why do you think *we* would help you?"

She raised her eyebrows in surprise. "That's the reason you're here. Why else would the Earth Mother have permitted you to reach here? If you weren't under her protection my disciples would have killed you. She let you pass through their ranks unmolested."

Wilson glanced down at the nozzle of the flame-thrower and then at the bloody spike Kimberley was holding. Jane had pointedly ignored both weapons. She refused to consider the possibility that they may have fought their way to her. Nothing could be allowed to shake her self-delusion of divinity. He decided the only course of action was to humor her, to let her keep believing that she was still in control of the situation, and that her followers were still alive.

He said, "And how could we help you?"

"I admit I was puzzled when you first entered. Because neither of you bear any sign of the Mother's embrace. But now, of course, I understand why. One of you is obviously immune—a simple test will tell me which one. I need another immune specimen for the final series of tests. My other specimen is of no further use to me. His tissues have been exhausted."

"What other specimen? Where is he?" demanded Wilson, looking around the room.

She ignored the question. "No doubt you will prove to be the immune one," she continued, pointing at Kimberley. "Barry's role will be to act as my assistant. After all, he was a mycologist." She shook her head in wonder. "How truly wise is the Earth Mother, sending me a trained laboratory technician at the crucial moment. And how fitting her choice in you, Barry. Though a man, you will be instrumental in her ultimate victory. Your final actions will atone a little for all the terrible sins of your sex against her. Just as your son also helped atone for his maleness."

"*Simon,*" he cried, taking a step toward her. "What the hell are you talking about? Where is he?"

She moved backward. "He's here, Barry. Come and see him. He's a glorious sight." She turned and walked over to a large glass cabinet into which a series of tubes were plugged. Wilson hurried after her, followed by Kimberley.

The other side of the cabinet was transparent. It was filled with something soft. Jane tapped the glass. The softness moved. In the midst of it a pair of eyes suddenly opened. They were bright blue.

"Our son," said Jane proudly.

Wilson stared into his son's eyes. They stared back imploringly. There was, Wilson saw with horror, still intelligence in them.

In a strangled voice Wilson said, "And Jessica? What have you done with her, you murdering bitch?"

"Jessica is fine," answered Jane, sounding puzzled by his reaction. "She is happy within the embrace of the Mother. She guards this sacred place with the rest of my followers. I'm surprised you didn't see her on the way up here."

Wilson dropped the nozzle of the fire extinguisher. It fell to the floor with a clatter as he spun round to face Jane. "Jessica was among those *creatures*?" he screamed.

She gazed at him calmly, her expression self-satisfied and smug. "All will be clear to you when the Mother finally takes you into her embrace," she told him, and gave a beatific smile.

He slammed his right fist into her mouth as hard as he could, following through with all his weight. He expected to knock her unconscious. He didn't expect her head to fly from her shoulders with a dry *snap*.

Kimberley screamed.

Headless, Jane's body tottered in front of him. No blood spurted from the end of the neck. Instead green fluid began to trickle out. He could see that her whole body was riddled on the inside with fungus.

The body, still upright, lurched past him, its arms flailing. Kimberley screamed again as it seemed to move straight for her. She struck out at it with her spiked rod. The make-shift spear went through Jane's chest without meeting any resistance and protruded from her back. Kimberley ran screaming away from it.

The thing lurched about for several more steps then fell, twitching, to the floor.

Wilson turned his back on it and stared once again at the shape which had been his son. "Simon," he said, helplessly. The blue eyes blinked.

He freed himself from the harness of the flame-thrower and let the hideous weapon drop with a crash. Then he bent down and began pulling the tubes out of the cabinet. Liquid spilled from them across the floor. He heard Kimberley approaching. She was crying.

"You killed her," she sobbed. "You killed her and now we'll never know the secret of her enzyme."

He said nothing. He pulled the rest of the tubes out of the cabinet, then stood again. As he hoped, the pair of blue eyes soon began to glaze over.

"Are you listening to me?" demanded Kimberley, grabbing him by the arm. "We've got no hope now of getting what we came for. You've ruined every . . ." She paused, then gasped, "Oh God, look!"

He turned and saw what had alarmed her.

It was Jane's head. It had rolled to the base of one of the nearby incubators and now, as it lay there, it was slowly cracking open.

Almost incuriously Wilson walked over to it. He gazed down at Jane's eyes, which were wide-open and startled-looking. A large fissure ran down her forehead to the bridge of her nose and as he watched the crack widened. Then suddenly the skull snapped entirely into two halves, revealing a white, spherical fungus. It continued to expand . . .

Kimberley cried, "Look, her body too!"

He turned and saw that Jane's headless corpse was undergoing a transformation as well. It was being shaken by a series of convulsions, as if it were trying to sit up. Then, from the stump of the neck, hyphae began to flow out and spread across the floor.

Wilson stood transfixed at the sight of his wife's corpse collapsing in upon itself. As the hyphae spread threateningly towards them Kimberley ran to the flame-thrower. She picked it up and tried to make it work. She finally figured out how to turn it on and yelped as flames roared out. Awkwardly she sprayed fire over the fungus radiating out of Jane's body, and then incinerated the head.

"How do I turn it off?" she cried in alarm as fire continued to gush from the nozzle. He was forced to go and assist her. But by the time he'd managed to switch it off it was too late. The laboratory was burning.

The fire caught hold very quickly, forcing them back toward the entrance. It was then that he noticed the small glass case sitting on a table that had been decorated to resemble an altar. Telling Kimberley to get out, he made a frantic dash through the flames to the case.

Sitting in the case was a pile of paper. On the top sheet he recognized the dense scrawl of Jane's handwriting. He had found her notes.

He snatched up the case and ran for the doorway. The flames licked at his bare skin, making him scream. And then, at last, he was through the doorway and safe.

8

Kimberley died three days later.

It was on the morning of the day after the fire that he noticed the small patch of bright orange mold behind her right knee. They had spent hours helping Carter carry his equipment across to the nearby Euston Tower, which he considered to be the best alternative location for his transmitter after the fire had completely gutted the Post Office Tower.

While Carter worked to rig his makeshift transmitter, utilizing the antenna and other undamaged equipment from the local radio station—Capital Radio—that had been based in the building, Wilson and Kimberley went exploring and found a tankful of water in a relatively untouched apartment near the top of the building.

It was a relief to be able to wash the encrusted blood and filth from their bodies, and despite his exhaustion and depression, Wilson responded to the sheer sensuality of the experience. As he helped wash Kimberley he felt a sudden and intense desire for her. By making love he would be able to blot out, if only for a short time, all the horrors of the last couple of days.

And it was soon obvious that she shared his mood—her body trembled under his touch as he rinsed the soapy water from her. But as he leaned down to raise another cupped handful of water from the bathtub he saw the small patch of orange.

"Kimberley," he sighed, all desire gone in that instant.

She looked down and followed the direction of his gaze. The only sound she made was a tiny, child-like, "Oh."

He hugged her, not knowing what to say. For a few moments she clung to him, then pushed him gently, but firmly, away. "Come on," she said in a steady voice, "we'd better go see how Carter is making out."

They didn't mention the fungus again that day, but by nightfall it was no longer possible to ignore it. By then her right leg, from foot to upper thigh, was covered in the orange mold. It was as if she were wearing a single woollen stocking.

Carter couldn't have helped noticing it but he said nothing either. They were sitting in what had been one of Capital Radio's control rooms. With his spare parts Carter had got some of the equipment functioning again and they had just completed making a recording of Wilson's analysis of Jane's notes. Wilson had quickly read through all the notes, knowing that once out of their sealed case the paper would quickly be attacked by the fungus. He had succeeded in pinpointing the vital information. He identified the crucial enzymes that had been modified, and then gave a detailed description of the chemical structure of Jane's resulting super-enzyme. Carter's intention was to put the tape on a loop and transmit it continuously.

It was then that Kimberley had asked Carter suddenly, "Do you think it's symbiotic or parasitic?" Both men knew what she was referring to.

"It's too early to tell," wheezed Carter.

She was thoughtful for a while, then said, "Well, at least it's prettier than some I've seen."

Carter began the transmission. As he was relying solely on batteries for power, he wasn't sure if the signal would carry far enough, nor did he have the means to build a receiver to hear if the signal was acknowledged.

"What are the chances?" Wilson asked him.

"Fifty-fifty. We're sending on the designated frequency, so someone somewhere should be monitoring it 24 hours a day waiting to hear from you. It all depends on how close to us the nearest functioning receiver is now. It may be that the fungus has spread right through Wales to the coast. Then again, how far a signal travels often varies depending on atmospheric conditions; so the longer I can keep this equipment functioning, the better our chances are."

Wilson and Kimberley left Carter in the dimly lit control room, anxiously tending the vulnerable transmitter. They returned to the apartment they'd found earlier. They knew there were some cans of food stored in a kitchen cupboard.

They ate in darkness on the floor of the living room, opening one can after another by touch and then tasting to identify the contents. It was a strange meal, consisting of asparagus tips, courgettes, tuna fish, tomato soup, apricot halves, rice pudding, and evaporated milk. They even managed to laugh at one point when Wilson realized he'd opened a can of dog food.

Afterward, by an unspoken agreement, they made love. In the darkness, on the floor, they made love with a frantic, desperate, urgency. At first he tried to avoid touching her right leg but soon it didn't matter to him, nor to her . . .

Later, as they lay in each other's arms, she sighed and said, "I wish now we'd got to know each other better." She spoke matter-of-factly and he realized she was now resigned to the fact of her imminent death.

He gave her a gentle hug. "So do I. But there's still time."

"Yes, I suppose so," she said but he knew she didn't mean it.

"For a start you could tell me why you came along on this trip. I know you've been hiding something all along."

She sighed again. "You're right. I had an ulterior motive. It made sense once but now it seems crazy. I would never have succeeded."

"In doing what?"

"In getting my parents out of prison. They were convicted last year in Johannesburg under the Anti-Terrorism Act, conspiring to cause explosions." She gave a bitter laugh. "It was all trumped up by the security boys, of course. My parents have had connections with anti-apartheid movements for years now, but they'd never be involved with violence. My mother's a doctor, for God's sake. But she's been sentenced to 10 years and my father to 15."

Wilson made a sympathetic sound though he couldn't see what possible link there might be between her parents' jail sentence and the fungus.

"When I heard what was happening in London," she continued, "and learned the reason for it, I came up with this wild scheme. It involved mutated lichen fungi—you know the special properties of lichen fungi, don't you?"

"Vaguely," he said, trying to remember. "I know they're a strange combination of fungi and algae."

"Yes, and they have the ability to absorb heavy metals. There's a theory that the gold deposits in South Africa at Witwatersrand are the result of lichen fungi in pre-Cambrian lagoons absorbing the gold out of the water. I had the idea of using mutated lichen fungi to extract gold in vast quantities from sea water. And if that was possible it would mean the ruination of the South African economy, because the price of gold would plummet and the country still depends on the damn stuff so much."

He understood now. "You were going to try and blackmail the South African government into setting your parents free."

"Yes."

"But it would have meant modifying Jane's mutating agent to the point where it was safe. That would have been very risky, and complicated."

He felt her shrug in his arms. "I was going to worry about that later. The main priority was to make sure your wife's secret wasn't lost. So I maneuvered myself into a position where I was indispensable to the mission."

He considered what she'd told him. "You *were* crazy," he said finally. "It would never have worked."

"Maybe not, but I had to try. Now I rather wish I hadn't . . . I'm not as strong as I thought I was. I don't want to die but I don't want to end up like all those other creatures."

He squeezed her. "Don't think about it. Not now."

But she continued, "Will you do me a favor?"

"Anything."

"If you survive all this, will you try to contact my parents and tell them about me?"

"Of course, *if* I survive. But I don't think much of my chances."

"No," she said seriously, "I'm certain you will get out of this uninfected. Your wife was right. One of us was naturally immune, but it wasn't me."

"I've just been lucky so far."

"No. It's probably genetic. Your son was immune, before your wife—" She paused. "I'm sorry."

He felt her lips brush his. "Promise me you'll do what I asked?" she whispered.

"Yes, I promise," he said and meant it. And he'd do his best to get her parents out of prison as well. As the man who—hopefully—helped save the world, he would be entitled to some rewards.

They made love again. More slowly this time, and with genuine affection. Then he fell asleep.

When he woke up bright daylight flooded the room and Kimberley was gone.

He knew in his heart it was a waste of time, but he searched for her anyway. He couldn't find her until he went out onto the roof and looked down. Far below, lying on yellow fungus that coated the sidewalk was a small splotch of bright orange.

His eyes stung as the hot tears filled them. Then he went back down to the control room.

Carter was asleep. The equipment didn't appear to be functioning. Wilson gently shook Carter awake and asked him what the situation was.

"I kept it going for over six hours," wheezed Carter, "but then some mold got into the works. We can only hope someone heard . . ." He looked around. "Where's the lady?"

"Kimberley's gone," said Wilson.

"I see," said Carter, his heavy head tilting forward.

The days passed monotonously. When Wilson wasn't scavenging for food and drink, he spent the time sitting on the roof of the Euston Tower with Carter. They were waiting for something to happen—a sign of some kind—though they didn't know what.

Carter didn't talk much anymore. He was finding it difficult to breathe due to the weight of the crust on his head, neck and chest.

During one of their last conversations Wilson said, "Christ, I could do with a cigarette."

"Bad for your lungs," wheezed Carter, and made his laughing sound. Then he said, "Me . . . I'd like to read a book. Anything at all. Even a Flannery novel."

Wilson laughed too.

On the eighth day they got their sign. It was near sunset and they were sitting in their customary place on the roof. Suddenly an RAF jet flew overhead with a thunderous roar. It circled low over the area, rocked its wings, and then disappeared to the north.

"You think that was an acknowledgment of our message?" Wilson asked eagerly.

"Had to be," wheezed Carter. "No other way they'd know we were here."

The next morning, Carter was dead. He'd suffocated in his sleep.

Wilson left him where he lay and by evening the fungus had consumed him completely. The bright orange stain on the sidewalk far below had long disappeared.

Every morning and night Wilson checked himself for the fungus, but he remained uninfected. Kimberley had been right, it seemed. He was immune. Not that it really seemed to matter any more.

A week or so after Carter's death he was sitting on the roof one late afternoon, drinking a bottle of wine he'd found, and staring vacantly out over the fungus-covered vista, when he heard a loud rumbling sound. He looked and saw the Post Office Tower starting to topple over. It fell toward Tottenham Court Road in slow motion, and when it hit the ground, after smashing through the brittle shells of the smaller buildings beneath it, the impact made the Euston Tower shake.

Wilson guessed that the fungus had finally eaten through the concrete base of the Post Office structure. He was glad it had collapsed. Every time he looked at it he remembered what its bulbous summit had contained . . . the horrors of Jane's laboratory . . . his son's eyes staring out of that cabinet.

For some reason he interpreted the destruction of the tower as an even more positive sign than the RAF jet's appearance.

All of a sudden he knew for certain that the battle would be won and the fungus would be destroyed.

He drank the rest of the wine and flung the bottle high into the air.

Milton Keynes UK
Ingram Content Group UK Ltd.
UKHW041310301023
431606UK00010B/143

9 781948 405164